EYE SPY

TAHIR SHAH

EYE SPY

TAHIR SHAH

MMXXII

Secretum Mundi Publishing Ltd
Kemp House
City Road
London
EC1V 2NX
United Kingdom

www.secretum-mundi.com
info@secretum-mundi.com

First published by Secretum Mundi Publishing Ltd, 2022
VERSION 26102021

EYE SPY

© TAHIR SHAH

Visit the author's website at:
Tahirshah.com

ISBN 978-1-912383-95-5

This book is for Minor Watt —
A little of whom lives in us all.

A photograph inspired me to write *Eye Spy*.

It showed a neat arrangement of prosthetic glass eyes. When I saw it for the first time, I couldn't stop looking at it, for it was both the most beautiful and the most repulsive thing I had ever seen.

I know next to nothing about surgery, and very little about eyes, and so it was impulsive of me to sit down to write a novel in which the protagonist is an eye surgeon — the greatest of his age.

I would ask therefore that you suspend reality for a short while, and allow me some liberties. I am hoping that the story fills you with delight and horrifies you in equal measure.

Tahir Shah

One

THE WAITING ROOM of Dr. Amadeus Kaine's practice was panelled in antique mahogany and smelled of Indian lemongrass.

The aroma was added to the air conditioning ducts twice weekly. It soothed the patients' nerves and transported their minds far away, to a realm beyond the rare and dignified landscape of the Upper East Side.

Drowning in awards and international acclaim, Dr. Kaine had made an art form out of ophthalmology — the study and treatment of conditions concerning the human eye. His services were in such demand that anyone without at least an A-grade referral was politely declined.

The stamp-cluttered pages of the surgeon's passport were testament to both his popularity and his extraordinary professional skill. Past clients included royalty, Nobel laureates, and presidents — a great many of them dictators from the former Soviet republics, from Latin America, and from Africa.

At 11.25 a.m. the buzzer sounded once, short and loud, and Mrs. Phelps, the receptionist, pressed the door release. Nearing retirement age, she was courteous yet a little brusque, her heavy, dark-rimmed glasses unsettling to some of the more anxious clients.

A minute and a half after the buzzer sounded, there was a knock on the door of suite 1005. A moment after that, a pair of bearded foreign gentlemen dressed in handmade woollen suits were standing to attention in front of Mrs. Phelps's desk.

One of them was slimmer than the other. Both had almond-shaped eyes and thick, fleshy faces, hefty in the jowls.

'We are here to see the doctor,' said the more slender of the men, his accent hard to place.

'And the name would be?'

'Drusnev… Vladimir Drusnev.'

Mrs. Phelps reached up with a clipboard and a pencil.

'Would you please fill this out, and give me full details of your condition, Mr. Drusnev?'

'I am not the patient,' said the man sternly.

'Then your friend. Could he complete the form?'

'But neither of us is Drusnev.'

'Oh, where exactly is Mr. Drusnev, then?'

'He is in Moslok.'

'*Mos*…?'

'*Lok*… Moslok… It is our capital.'

The heavier of the men leaned up to the desk. He was so close that Mrs. Phelps could clearly see the individual strands of bristle beneath his nose.

'Drusnev,' he said very slowly. 'He is our president.'

'Ah, I see.'

The doctor's assistant pressed a miniature brass buzzer on the underside of her desk. Then she pressed it again long and hard, signifying the arrival of a VIP client.

'You had better go in,' she said.

Two

DR. KAINE WAS standing with his back to the desk, a delicate Limoges coffee cup in his right hand, his eyes fixed out on the street. The cup was empty, and had been for five minutes. But the doctor hadn't noticed. He was watching a plastic bag as it was tossed up on the winter eddies and swirls.

Behind him, the spacious examination room was quite silent, except for the tick-tick-tick of a mantel clock. In the magnificent world of Kaine's imagination, the London Symphony Orchestra was accompanying the melodrama of the plastic bag on its journey uptown, with a movement from Wagner's *Ring*.

Born on Manhattan, and educated privately on the East Coast, Amadeus Kaine was an Anglophile through and through. All his suits were tailored at Huntsman in London's Savile Row, and his shoes were made by Tricker's, where he had his own maple lasts. His white shirts were the finest English muslin, made to measure like everything else. As for his citrus aftershave, it was specially concocted for him by Taylor's, another Jermyn Street favourite.

Kaine was a long lean man, standing six foot two and a half. His shoulders were broad, his hands impressively wide, the nails expertly manicured. He was fifty-three but could have passed for a man a decade younger, his bottle-green eyes bright and mischievous, and his slender face capable of conjuring expressions of extreme gravity.

The buzzer sounded a second time.

5

Kaine blinked. Resting the Limoges cup on the desk's walnut veneer, he thought of that evening's meeting. The first Tuesday of the month meant it was the rendezvous of the Obscure Cuisine Dining Club, of which he was a proud member.

It was his night to host.

His ears having picked up the faint sound of a brass door handle turning, he smiled.

In the twenty-five years of his Madison Avenue practice, almost the greatest thrill for Kaine was meeting a new client for the first time. And the surgeon prided himself on his ability to size up anyone in the dozen paces between the door and the desk. Poised like an eagle, he would watch in silence as they entered before moving towards him.

The door opened and the two bearded gentlemen from Moslok paced in a hesitant diagonal across the room.

Kaine noticed their overcoats first — fine cloth, well tailored and probably French, leading down to equally expensive English shoes. Their ties were high end, too, undoubtedly Hermès, as was the pair of matching alligator attaché cases.

The doctor took in the faces last.

He believed that a costume and the way it was carried could reveal so much more than a few inches of skin on the front of the head. Both men were rather weatherworn and unloved, as though they were executives in a more powerful man's employ. Even before they had opened their mouths, Kaine had come to the conclusion they were seeking a service for someone who had risen fast to power, and retained it with an iron grasp.

The pair stood to attention on the far side of the desk. The slender one dipped his head in respect, his expression so serious as to appear alarming.

'We have come from Moslok in the Republic of Bhochnivia,' he said, 'on the orders of His Excellency President Vladimir Drusnev.'

Dr. Kaine spat out a greeting, then scribbled half a line of words with a 2H pencil on a memorandum pad.

'May I enquire about the nature of his condition?'

The thicker-built visitor opened his attaché case, removed a single sheet of paper, and slid it across the walnut veneer.

Kaine scanned it, his eyes narrowing.

'It seems as though a ciliarotomy has been advised,' he said. 'I would be more than happy to examine President Drusnev. When would it be possible for him to come in?'

The first of the henchmen shook his head.

'Drusnev is too busy to travel,' he said, a touch of loathing in his voice.

'That's a pity.'

'We will take you to him instead.'

The second henchman tapped his watch, a monstrous gold Rolex.

'We leave tomorrow.'

'We will fly direct to Moslok.'

'Our aeroplane will be ready early.'

Kaine touched a fingertip to his lips in thought. He liked travel, especially to obscure Central Asian republics. The raw cultures appealed to him, as did the opportunity to indulge in obscure carnivorous gastronomy, his greatest passion of all.

'What medical facilities do you have available in...'

'*Moslok.*'

'In Moslok?'

The slender henchman gave a thumbs up.

'Very good!' he exclaimed.

The second of the men opened his attaché case once again. He pulled out a brick of hundred-dollar bills and dropped it with a thump on the desk.

'We leave at sunrise,' he said.

Three

THE OBSCURE CUISINE Dining Club comprised six middle-aged men and was dedicated to fare regarded as peculiar or outlandish in normal society. All the members were, like Amadeus Kaine, high-flying leaders in their fields.

Two were investment bankers who had done well despite Wall Street's recent rollercoaster ride. A third was in aviation, a fourth was a film director, and the fifth a bestselling novelist. They had all been friends for decades and knew the intimate details of each other's lives.

Best of all though, was the fact they weren't out to impress each other — except on occasions when they were hosting the dining club. Each member had two opportunities a year to cook a meal. Their offering was rated on a scale graded one to five. In the club's history there had been plenty of threes and even fours, but no one had ever achieved full marks.

The month before, Herbert Hoffman, the novelist, had hosted. His meal had been a feast of such epicurean extravagance that it had scored a four and a half — only the second repast in the club's eighty-year history to have done so.

The *pièce de résistance* of Hoffman's coup was a scorpion bisque flavoured with white truffles from Provence.

The thought of creating anything that could compete with it thrust Kaine into an anxious state of melancholy.

For two weeks he had spent every available moment considering the menu and sourcing ingredients. Many hours had been spent crisscrossing the by-lanes of Chinatown on the trail of something fabulous and unusual.

One evening the week before, having given up hope, he was about to head back to his apartment when a wizened old man selling Kazakh pork bellies directed him to a warehouse on Bayard Street. Somewhere near the back, in dim light, a blind man was peddling a variety of curious ingredients from a series of small barrels. They included sea slugs, large orange starfish, pickled shark's hearts, and a hard cheese infested with insect larvae.

Dr. Kaine bought three pounds of the slugs and began experimenting with them. He found that their natural taste could be enhanced with an infusion of fermented lime juice and vintage Calvados.

Nothing in life fascinated the surgeon quite so much as the search for the perfect marriage of taste and consistency. Rather obsessive by nature, he kept a small Smythson notebook to hand, in which he documented the taste and consistency of all food that passed his lips.

That evening, at a quarter to eight, the members of the dining club began arriving at Kaine's apartment, on the sixth floor of 775 Park Avenue. They made small talk for a while, and clinked their flutes of Pol Roger together, toasting the meal to follow. Their host was regarded as a perfectionist as well as a gourmet, a point that only raised the sense of communal anticipation.

Two hours earlier, Kaine had judged the first batch of sea slugs to be ruined, having given it a little too much brandy. Enraged at his own stupidity, he had raced out to the street, hailed a cab, and directed it to the gloomy warehouse down in Chinatown.

Fortunately, the blind man still had a considerable stock. No one else, it seemed, had an interest in sea slugs. But, sensing the customer's enthusiasm for the product, he doubled the price.

At eight-thirty p.m. the members took their seats, charged their glasses with a good Saint-Émilion, and declared their solemn oath to their fraternity.

'Gentlemen,' said Kaine after a long pause, 'I have struggled to create a dish that might come close to the delight experienced at our last rendezvous. And what a struggle it has been!'

A wave of courteous laughter rippled through the room. It was followed by the sound of gentle muttering. A moment later, an *amuse-bouche* was brought out by the maid — a nugget of reindeer pâté from Lapland, served on a sliver of green fig.

Following tradition, Kaine gave a toast to Walter B. Smisstein, the founder of the dining club. Then, in line with another tradition, he took a nibble at the pâté to prove it wasn't a danger to human health. The custom of sampling one's offering first came about in June 1948, after an elderly member of the club expired mid-meal, struck down by suspect shellfish.

The five guests swallowed their reindeer, and each of them praised its distinct meaty tang. One of the bankers, Frederick Barton, who was to host the next month, made a joke about Rudolph, but no one laughed. They were far too intrigued by what Kaine had prepared for the main course. But before it was served, there came a pungent starfish consommé, itself accompanied by homemade beef-bread.

Fresh glasses were brought out, and a second red wine poured. An Australian Montara, it was dark and fruity, the vines having been ripened on the eastern slopes of Mount Chalambar.

Only when the wine had been tasted by one and all were the plates of sea slug served. Pea green, congealed, and lightly fragrant, the dish was unlike anything that had been served in the dining club's history.

'Interesting,' said the film director. 'It reminds me of tripe.'

'Looks like you've surpassed yourself,' muttered the pilot.

'What is it?' asked a third.

Kaine took a sip of Montara and allowed the liquid to swill around his mouth. He disliked conversing when eating, even with close friends. As far as he was concerned, conversation adversely affected the taste buds.

'You all know,' he said, in a slow deliberate voice, 'that I have searched for an eternity to find the perfect blend of texture and taste. Well, I think that at last, gentlemen, I may have succeeded in achieving my goal.'

The surgeon raised his glass, toasted the health of the fraternity once again, and said, 'I give you *limaces de mer au Calvados*, sea slugs in brandy.'

He took a spoonful of the dish and, following his lead, the other members dug in.

Within a few minutes all the plates were wiped clean and every tongue was describing the taste in superlatives.

Dessert came next.

A rich layered trifle, it was infused with a curious milk-like liquid from the Upper Amazon known as *masato*. Creamy and mildly intoxicating, it had been produced from the fermentation of masticated manioc roots. Kaine refused to reveal the source for his supply, although it was noted that his maid's jaw was bandaged on one side.

After the meal, the members of the fraternity cast their votes.

By popular acclaim Kaine was awarded four and three-quarter points. While maintaining a sombre veneer, he thanked his guests for their generosity.

But inside he was dancing.

Four

By THE TIME the commuters of Madison Avenue were getting in to work the next morning, the Gulfstream G650 was cruising at 38,000 feet in the direction of Bhochnivia.

At LaGuardia, formalities had been minimal.

The bullet-proof black Mercedes of President Drusnev's henchmen had been waved through three security posts, and had then been escorted right up to the plane.

Amadeus Kaine was quite used to the world of the super-rich, a realm in which private jets were one of many perks. As he ascended the steps, his luggage was loaded aboard, and he was soon sipping a glass of chilled Taittinger Champagne.

Uncertain of the president's exact condition, or the facilities on offer to treat him, the surgeon had packed a considerable array of equipment. There was no question of exceeding the limit. Indeed, as Kaine had learned over the years, when it came to dictators, the more demanding one was, the more seriously one was taken.

The flight of just over twelve hours gave the surgeon time to relax from the festivities of the evening before, as well as to read up on Bhochnivia. Asking the pretty young stewardess for a couple of extra pillows, Kaine pushed them into the small of his back. A skiing accident five years earlier had left him with chronic back pain, one that no amount of medication could cure.

Back to the Wikipedia entry on Bhochnivia.

The doctor had learned that the republic was a former Soviet territory, that it was abundant in gas, oil, and opals, and that it was about the size of Moldova. The coat of arms bore a four-headed griffin and was emblazoned on a background of deep blue to form the national flag. A quick browse of the Human Rights Watch site had confirmed

Kaine's suspicions — that Bhochnivia was an autocracy of the most deplorable kind.

Vladimir Drusnev was leader of the only party. He and his family owned everything from the country's oil and gas concessions to its vast mineral reserves. Anyone daring to speak out against Drusnev was disappeared — taken to the opal mines, from which they never returned. The jails were, it was said, as full to capacity as the shelves of the shops were empty.

The privileged elite — all of whom were related to the president — had private jets at their disposal for shopping jaunts to Moscow, Paris, or Beijing.

At Drusnev International, the Gulfstream landed into the wind, and taxied slowly up to the end of a long red carpet. The engines powered down and, as they did so, the door was opened and Kaine climbed down.

The president's chief of staff was waiting on the tarmac.

With as much pomp and ceremony as he could muster, he welcomed the distinguished surgeon to the Republic of Bhochnivia and invited him to inspect the guard of honour, as a film crew from the local BTV captured the spectacle.

Ten minutes later, Amadeus Kaine was sitting back in a silver Rolls-Royce Phantom as it sped fast through the suburbs of Moslok. Out of the windows he couldn't help but notice the sprawling shantytowns and squalor, the kind that forms a dark and shameful balance to extreme wealth. From time to time they would pass another limousine, the windows blacked out, the chauffeur and passengers oblivious to the shoeless pedestrians outside.

The vehicle made a beeline straight to the presidential palace, where the guards saluted and then presented arms.

'His Excellency is waiting for you in the Throne Room,' said the chief of staff in a sour tone.

'I should like to have my equipment brought through,' Kaine replied, 'although I assume we shall not be doing any surgery today.'

'The surgery shall be carried out when His Excellency wishes. Do you understand?'

The surgeon nodded. Experience had taught him that, when in a Central Asian dictatorship, it paid dividends to go with the flow and never to attempt to call the shots.

The Rolls came to a halt.

As soon as it was stationary, the doors were opened by a team of officers in golden uniforms, matching capes pinned to their backs. The visitor was invited to scale a marble staircase strewn with rose petals. He counted them as he went — sixty steps, one for each of the president's years.

Despite having treated dictators and potentates the world over, not to mention a *Who's Who* of Hollywood celebrity, Dr. Kaine had never set eyes on such astonishingly horrifying kitsch.

Almost every surface was overlaid in twenty-four carat gold.

There were gold vases as tall as palm trees, vast marble fountains and colonnades, arched doorways, and chandeliers the size of family cars. The floors were marble, too, shrouded with exquisite geometric rugs. As for the doors, they were solid gold.

'This way, please,' said an equerry striding up fast. 'The supreme leader is waiting next door.' He paused, took a deep breath, and said: 'The president dislikes being touched, and so please refrain from shaking hands, or achieving actual contact of any kind.'

'That will be difficult if I am to examine him.'

'Well… do your best to do it from a distance.'

The solid gold doors were pulled apart, and Kaine got his first glimpse of the Throne Room. It was so large that he drew breath fearfully.

A dark, burly figure was standing in the middle of the room, as though he was somehow set on dominating the space. His face was brutish and rough, that of a gangster who had clawed his way up from the gutters. He was wearing patent leather riding boots with solid gold spurs, and a blood-red uniform, the chest entirely hidden in medals.

Flexing his shoulder blades and gritting his teeth, he waited for Amadeus Kaine to approach.

'Welcome to my country!' he boomed.

'Thank you, Your Excellency.'

'Your journey… it is good?'

'Very much so.'

'Good.'

Drusnev wiped a hand over his left eye, leaving the fingers moist with tears.

The surgeon lowered his head in a bow.

'I am at your disposal to examine you when you wish, Your Excellency,' he said.

The president flexed his shoulder blades a second time.

It was clear he disliked being thought of as ailing. He clicked his fingers twice, whereupon a partition wall descended electronically, revealing a full medical unit on the far side of the Throne Room.

'We have hospital here,' he said.

Doing his best to keep his distance, Dr. Kaine made an initial examination of the eye, and saw that lacrimal drainage surgery was required.

'I shall need a little time to prepare. If it is convenient, I could complete the surgery this afternoon.'

Drusnev winced.

'It will be painful?' he whispered.

'Not terribly so,' said Kaine.

The president wiped his eye once again.

'You are very good doctor, no?' he said.

Five

THE OPERATION ITSELF took fifteen minutes and was a complete success. Mindful that he had to be seen to earn his substantial fee, Kaine fussed about in the makeshift operating theatre for eight times as long. Checking gauges and examining computerized readouts, he strained to appear busy, alert, and in charge.

Despite this, his mind wasn't on the operation at all.

The procedure was so simple that the most junior of surgeons could have performed it. Instead, Kaine was thinking about the Bhochnivian national dish which he had read about — a bloated pig's stomach stuffed with day-old chicks.

As soon as the operation was over, news of the president's successful treatment and his courageousness on the table spread through the streets of Moslok and far beyond.

Ordinary people arrived at the palace with gifts of money and livestock — far more than any of them could afford. Mothers wept on the steps of government buildings, and their children waved little banners they had made at home. The national anthem blared from loudspeakers on every street corner, and the imperial guard marched up and down through the streets.

In public all were joyful that the supreme leader was back to health.

Sitting in his suite at the Moslok Sheraton, Amadeus Kaine watched it all on Bhochnivia TV. As with most tin-pot dictatorships, it was clear the general populace would have been coerced into putting on the frenzied celebrations. Kaine cursed himself for having colluded with yet another despot, and a particularly depraved one at that. But, sipping a miniature Jack Daniel's from the bottle, he congratulated himself as well.

As he did so, there was a knock at the door.

He opened it to find an imperial messenger, dressed in a flowing golden tunic, holding a purple scroll.

'A state banquet is to be held in your honour, Your Excellence,' he announced.

The surgeon did his best to seem pleased.

'When is it, the banquet?' he asked.

'Tomorrow night, Your Excellence, at eight o'clock.'

'Please extend my thanks to the supreme leader and say that I will be honoured and most humbled to attend.'

The messenger took a step back so that he could bow very deeply. When he was vertical again, he clapped his hands. As if from nowhere, a factotum appeared. He passed the messenger a small, gold presentation box, borne on a salver.

'The president would be pleased for you to accept this as a token of his gratitude,' he said.

'What is it?'

'A Bhochnivian delicacy.'

The messenger and his attendant disappeared, and Kaine stepped back into his room. He opened the box with curiosity and found a little pastry inside. It was sprinkled with what looked like icing sugar, and was unusually heavy for its diminutive size.

He sniffed it, but there was no obvious smell.

I'm beginning to like Bhochnivia, he thought to himself, taking a bite.

Beneath the thin layer of pastry lay a succulent interior, moist but not overly so. Kaine chewed ponderingly and, as he did so, a kaleidoscope of flavour tantalized his senses.

He took a second bite.

It was even more delicious than the first. His mind reeling, and his taste buds tingling, he flopped on the couch.

'This is it,' he exclaimed in a whisper. 'The most perfect food in the world!'

Six

THE NEXT MORNING it rained and the streets of Moslok glinted like cut glass, reflecting the myriad of banners, bunting, and the multitude of portraits featuring the supreme leader.

At 9.15 a.m., President Drusnev went on state television. He proclaimed that, as a gesture of goodwill, he would be releasing a dozen prisoners, and would provide free bread from his own kitchens to those schoolchildren most in need. An animated and impromptu discourse followed in which the president condemned what he called 'subversive forces' set on overthrowing his benevolent rule.

The oration lasted four and a half hours.

As soon as it had finished, the speech was repeated in case anyone had missed it the first time around. All other programmes were cancelled. But it didn't seem to worry anyone. After all, as the only television channel, BTV rarely broadcast anything that wasn't a celebration of President Drusnev's glorious reign.

After breakfast, a tailor arrived at Kaine's suite and measured him for evening dress, white tie and tails. An Albanian, he had learned his trade in the service of Nicolae Ceausescu, before being disgraced for pricking the secretary general's finger with a pin during a late-night fitting.

Standing there in a shirt and boxer shorts, Kaine cocked his head up to the presidential portrait on the room's far wall.

'What's he really like?' he asked delicately.

'He's a good man, sir, very loved by the people.'

'By all of them?'

The tailor ran the edge of his tape down the American's inside leg.

'Yes, sir.'

'Are you sure?'

'He is loved by all Bhochnivians,' he said firmly. 'Even by those who have not yet been born.'

Seven

BEFORE LUNCH, THE surgeon slipped out of his suite and made his way down to the hotel foyer. He had hoped to have the chance of wandering the streets alone, to soak up the atmosphere of Moslok, and to sample a few more culinary delicacies.

But no sooner had the elevator doors opened than a line of a dozen dignitaries stepped forward in greeting. Some of them bowed. All of them smiled.

'Your limousine is awaiting, Your Excellence,' said the first, a presidential aide-de-camp.

'Where will it take me?'

'On a tour.'

'A tour of what?'

'Of the marvels.'

Amadeus Kaine frowned.

'Which marvels would those be?'

'The marvels of the president's realm.'

A five-hour excursion followed in a procession of bullet-proof Range Rovers, escorted front and back by police outriders. All the while, the aide-de-camp spewed facts and superlatives, in an effort to remind Dr. Kaine of the supreme leader's imperial might.

They visited the National Monument, the centrepiece of which was a statue of Drusnev fashioned from pure platinum. There were real sapphires in the eye sockets, and pigeon-blood rubies made up the lips. When Kaine asked how such a precious sculpture could remain so intact, the aide-de-camp held a hand up to the sky.

'In Bhochnivia there is no crime!' he bellowed.

'None at all? How can that be?'

The officer glanced at the ground sheepishly.

'Because of the great adoration of the president,' he said.

After the National Monument came the imperial riding stables, where a performance of dressage just happened to be underway. A visit to a school came next, where the children sang the national anthem, before running out onto their central quad.

The surgeon was taken to look out from an upper floor classroom. Peering down, he saw that the children had spontaneously arranged themselves into the shape of the president's face. The fact that their various uniforms managed to create Drusnev so perfectly suggested that the next generation had cause to practise the feat often, and had been specially attired to do so.

The aide-de-camp had tears in his eyes.

'They love him so,' he said.

As the cortège of Range Rovers left the school, the children sang the anthem once again, and the vehicles purred away through silent streets to the next rendezvous.

It came in the form of a farmers' market on the outskirts of town. The place was pristine. All the stalls looked as though they had been styled for a film shoot, the produce and the people attending them immaculate.

The women were dressed in embroidered aprons, their hair tied back with ribbons, and the men were wearing prim tunics, the hems of which were lined with colourful brocade.

Kaine was invited to taste a local apple. It was crunchy and flavoursome, and somehow reminded him of the delicious pastry he had tasted the evening before. As they strolled through the market, ordinary citizens drifted about almost as though a movie director had shouted 'Action!'

Whenever Kaine attempted to deviate from the predetermined path, someone or something happened to block the way, and he was corralled to walk forward.

Unable to get the pastry out of his mind, he asked whether he might purchase some. The aide-de-camp's expression froze. He swallowed hard.

'They are reserved for the president and his guests,' he said sternly, leading the way back to the car.

In the afternoon, the fitting took place. The tailor had excelled himself; no alterations were required.

At six p.m., Kaine made a short examination of the president's eye. When it was over, an equerry briefed him on the formalities of the evening.

'You are to be presented with the Imperial Order of the Diamond Cross,' he said, 'Bhochnivia's highest civilian honour. After you have received it, you must kiss the right wrist of the president, signifying eternal servitude. After the ceremony, the banquet will begin.'

The equerry looked hard at Kaine, as though uncertain how to deliver difficult news.

'There will be fourteen courses,' he said, 'one for each year of the president's reign. The dishes, they…' the official swallowed hard as the aide-de-camp had done. 'They are sometimes regarded as unusual by visitors,' he said.

Amadeus Kaine raised an eyebrow.

'Unusual?'

'A little different.'

'Well, I am hoping to taste again the mouth-watering pastry that was brought to me last night.'

The equerry seemed to breathe easier.

'Oh yes,' he said assuredly, 'I can guarantee you will be dining on a great many more of those tonight.'

Eight

HELD IN THE Great Drusnev Hall of the People, the banquet was attended by almost a thousand guests. They had been drawn from the ranks of the new nobility, the elite of the burgeoning armed forces, and from the few diplomatic missions to have representatives in Bhochnivia. All the guests were clothed in their finest formal attire.

The ladies of the supreme leader's extended family were awash with tiaras and gems, the chests of the military were obscured by medals, and the ambassadorial costumes were adorned with silk sashes and magnificent decorations.

Amadeus Kaine had been amused by the world according to Drusnev, but he was now ready to leave. He had asked for the jet to be made ready at dawn so that he might, as he put it, cease to be a burden on the president's gracious hospitality.

Making note of his request, the secretary of state said he would seek the advice of the supreme leader when the appropriate moment arose.

In advance of the banquet, the presentation took place.

Dressed in imperial robes woven from genuine gold thread, President Drusnev moved slowly towards a podium that had been arranged at the far end of the hall. The extraordinary weight of the attire made his movements slow and clumsy.

One or two members of the audience wondered whether he was drunk. Naturally, they refrained from mentioning it, even to their spouses. After all, like all top-notch dictatorships, Bhochnivia was held together by a spider's web of informants and secret police.

The president tapped a fingertip to the microphone and silence prevailed at once.

'We people of Bhochnivia pleased,' he said in a commanding tone, 'to have Mr. Excellence Professor Kaine from New York-land. And, we people of Bhochnivia, give big honour to Mr. Excellence Professor Kaine. We people give him Imperial Order of Diamond Cross.'

A cheer resounded through the Great Hall and, on cue, Amadeus Kaine stepped forward. Struggling under the weight of his golden sleeves, the president pinned the medal onto the American surgeon's chest. Then he presented him with an orb on a stand. About the size of a tennis ball, it was inscribed with the name of every hamlet, village and town in the realm.

Having given thanks, once and then a second time, Kaine remembered to kiss the right presidential wrist, although it seemed like a strange thing to do.

Drusnev then nodded to his chief of staff, who signalled to the aide-de-camp, who in turn waved discreetly to the officer in charge of banquets.

A moment of silence passed in which everyone present feared that a long and patriotic discourse might be about to begin. But, thankfully, a troop of liveried heralds stepped forward and proclaimed the commencement of the banquet.

Once the president and his guest of honour had taken their places at the head of the elongated table, the dignitaries filed mutely to their seats. Few of them wanted to be there, but they all knew very well that failing to respond to an invitation to dine at a state banquet was tantamount to signing one's own death warrant. There was nothing that riled the Supreme Leader more than when his family or his citizens failed to obey his wishes.

Thirteen courses followed, each one more odd than the last.

The meal began with white ant eggs in a fatty yak-meat gravy and was followed by lambs' brains in caviar. After that there were a range of delicacies that included silkworm larvae, stewed duck gizzards, and poached frogs' heads.

The president seemed to relish everything set before him. It was no surprise, of course, as he had chosen the menu himself. From time to time, he patted the air in front of him, declaring with a sparkle in his eye, 'Best food still to come!'

Other than the supreme leader, the only man at the table who was actually enjoying the meal was the eye surgeon. As a true gourmet, he was quite willing to try anything once, and was thrilled by culinary experimentation. Between each course he scribbled a comment in his Smythson notebook, which he kept discreetly on his lap.

As the plates of the thirteenth course were removed by the legions of serving staff, a hush fell over the room. Assuming that their president was about to make an address, Kaine looked at Drusnev, who was seated adjacent to him.

'Now best of best… best of Bhochnivia!' he bellowed.

A throng of servants swept out from the kitchens, bearing salvers made from solid gold. The dishes were so heavy that they were borne to the banquet table by specially trained valets, some of whom doubled as athletes in the national Olympic team.

Kaine swivelled round.

To his surprise and sheer delight, the golden salvers were covered in the very same pastries that he had sampled the night before.

A pair of them was put before the American, and he wasted no time in devouring them.

Overcome with pleasure that his guest appreciated the dish, Drusnev shrugged.

'You like?' he asked energetically.

'I adore them!' Amadeus Kaine declared. 'They are quite unlike anything I have ever tasted. So moist, so firm, so subtle in their kaleidoscopic taste.'

The president clapped his hands and a golden tray of the pastries was laid before the American.

'Eat more!' he said.

'Thank you, thank you! I certainly will.'

Seated beside the surgeon, the president's aide-de-camp pushed the pastry served to him around his plate with a golden fork. He was perspiring, as if greatly vexed. The supreme leader jabbed a finger at his plate and then at his mouth.

'You not eat?' he hissed.

The officer broke off a corner and shovelled it through his lips, chewing halfheartedly.

Kaine watched.

Then, glancing down the table, he noticed that almost every guest had left their pastries. He didn't understand why. After all, the delicacy brought him more pleasure than anything he had ever tasted.

'Your Excellency,' he said, making the most of the silence, 'I would be fascinated to know what exactly these extraordinary pastries contain.'

The aide-de-camp seemed to perspire all the more. He put down his fork and waited for the president's reply.

Plucking one of the smaller tartlets from the platter, Drusnev swallowed it whole, without chewing. He wiped a hand boisterously over his mouth, belched, and exclaimed:

'My honour… to serve my people and to get rare food. *This* rare food. Rarest food. Secret food. Not in your country. Only in Bhochnivia!'

The eye surgeon was intrigued. Leaning forward discreetly, he asked:

'And what exactly would the secret ingredient be, Your Excellency?'

President Drusnev sucked his upper lip. He grinned, wiped his mouth again, and didn't seem so much nervous as guarded.

'Magical food,' he said, 'heals the body food. Very very good.'

The supreme leader gave a double thumbs up, and Dr. Kaine shrugged.

'I beg you, please tell me what it is.'

The supreme leader strained to look meek.

'You think me naughty,' he said.

'Naughty? Surely not. No, no, that would be impossible, Your Excellency.'

The president let out a high-pitched little giggle.

'Inside pastries is Bhochnivia people eyes,' he said.

Nine

AMADEUS KAINE DIDN'T sleep a wink that night.

All he could think of was that he had descended into a state of cannibalism, and how publicly reviled he would now be. He thanked providence that the only diplomats present were representatives of other tin-pot dictatorships, and none from anywhere near his own homeland.

The thought of having cooked human eyes moving through his intestinal tract was almost too much to bear. Returning to the suite at the Moslok Sheraton after the banquet, he decided to force himself to throw up.

He padded into the bathroom and stuck his fingers down the back of his throat but, curiously, nothing came up, except for a sludgy grey residue. So he slugged down a couple of JD miniatures, followed by a little bottle of Grand Marnier.

Then he sat on the couch and let out the deepest sigh of his life. What would the boys of the Obscure Cuisine Dining Club make of his experience? He spat out a chuckle at the thought of it, and at the irony that he, a celebrated ophthalmologist, had found human eyes quite so delicious as he had.

The next morning, Kaine was showered by six.

Although he hadn't slept, he felt totally invigorated. The ever-present pain in his back had disappeared, and his face seemed flushed, as though somehow a decade younger than the day before. He put the transformation down to the high altitude of Moslok and made a note to sing its praises as a tourist destination when he reached home.

The president's aide-de-camp knocked at the door of his suite a little after nine. There had been no effort to make the presidential jet available before then. It seemed that President Drusnev was reluctant to allow his distinguished visitor to leave.

'His Excellency was most pleased by your enthusiasm at the banquet last night,' said the officer. 'He has enquired whether you would not go hunting with him in the forest. An expedition is being prepared, and shall leave the day after next.'

'I'm a terrible shot,' said Kaine quickly. 'And I don't really like guns.'

The president's aide-de-camp seemed disheartened.

'His Excellency so enjoys interesting gentlemen such as yourself on a shoot,' he said.

'Out of interest,' said the surgeon, 'what would we be hunting?'

The officer looked down at his boots. The tips were expertly polished and shone like mirrors.

'Prisoners,' he said apologetically.

'*Prisoners?*'

The aide-de-camp nodded.

'They are released into the great forest and given a day or so to run before the hunting party sets out.'

'I really must be getting back to New York urgently,' Dr. Kaine replied, lying. 'You see, there's a matter I have to sort out with my ex-wife. She's causing a lot of trouble. I wonder if I might perhaps return another time for the hunt.'

The aide-de-camp perked up a little.

'That would be very good,' he said.

Kaine couldn't leave Moslok without knowing the truth about the mysterious pastries. He beckoned the officer into his suite.

'There's something I need to ask you,' he said.

'Yes, sir?'

'At the banquet last night, President Drusnev told me that the pastries were a national delicacy of Bhochnivia, that they are prepared using human eyes.' Kaine drew breath sharply. He paused. 'I must have misheard him,' he said.

The aide-de-camp looked down at his boots again, as his mind searched for a suitable answer.

'In Bhochnivia we have many ancient traditions,' he said, 'and one of the oldest is to consume certain body parts of our foes.'

'They were made from the eyes of your enemies?' asked Kaine.

'Sometimes that is the case. But we have not had the fortune of capturing any of late, and so the pastries you consumed were prepared with the eyes of prisoners.'

'And where are they kept, these prisoners?'

'In the opal mines,' replied the aide-de-camp.

Ten

TWO DAYS AFTER quitting Bhochnivia, Amadeus Kaine was back in his office, with Mrs. Phelps buzzing in yet another VIP client. Time and again he got flashes of the banquet and found himself imagining the mines in which eyeless prisoners were forced to toil.

On the flight back to New York, he had probed for more information about President Drusnev's unusual taste in patisserie. The bearded henchmen who accompanied him on the return journey to America were not forthcoming. All they would say was that the supreme leader was never misguided, and that if he felt it necessary to dine on prisoners' eyes, then it was surely his right to do so.

On the evening he reached his apartment, Kaine took a long, satisfying shower. He liked to run through his rituals in private, as though they somehow kept the Earth in orbit. First, he soaped his body with his right hand, and then with the left. After that, he scrubbed his fingernails one at a time while counting to fifty.

Once out of the shower, he applied cold cream to his hands and feet, got into his pyjamas, and brushed his teeth. All the while he counted. It was a habit he had picked up in early childhood, and one that had become increasingly dominant in recent years. The counting — usually in multiples of three, six or nine — calmed him and aided concentration.

Standing there in front of the bathroom mirror, Kaine looked casually at his face, while his lips mumbled multiples of six. His complexion was as bright and vital as it had been twenty years before. He examined it slowly, stretching the skin with his fingers.

Releasing it, he found that his cheek fell back into place instantly, with the elasticity of a young man's. And, turning his head, he noticed that the bald patch at the back, which he combed over so assiduously each morning, was entirely gone.

The next evening Kaine arranged to meet his old friend Herbert Hoffman for a drink or two at their club, the Metropolitan, a block from Central Park. They sat in the bar on low leather chairs, exchanging pleasantries before moaning about their ex-wives. Then, all of a sudden, Kaine leant forwards and touched the novelist on the knee.

'Since our little dinner the other night,' he said, 'I've had the strangest experience. I was invited to a Central Asian republic to operate on the leader.'

'Which one was it — Kazakhstan?'

'No, no, it was called Bhochnivia.'

'Never heard of it,' said Hoffman.

'Neither had I.'

'Sounds like a third-world autocracy to me.'

'That's just what it is,' replied Kaine. 'But the president's guilty of not only barbarity but astonishingly bad taste. There's all the usual bling bling you get in dictatorships.' The surgeon sipped his vodka tonic and looked over at his friend. 'But there was something else,' he said. 'Something I hadn't experienced before.'

Herbert Hoffman shifted in his chair, uncrossing his legs.

'What?'

'Cannibalism,' said Kaine, pronouncing the word flatly without any intonation.

'*Cannibalism?*'

'Yes. The president delights in it. He has little pastries filled with human eyes.'

'How disgusting,' said the novelist quickly. 'We should go in and set his people free!'

Kaine sipped his drink and looked across the room. He had wanted to tell Hoffman that he himself had tasted the human meat, that he had found it more delectable than anything that had ever passed his lips. But he dared not.

After all, the Obscure Cuisine Dining Club was one thing, but cannibalism was another.

It was the last taboo.

Eleven

THE NEXT MORNING, Kaine repaired to the small laboratory located behind his office. There was none of the old-world grandeur in there, just white ceramic tiles, bright strip-lighting, and the severe scent of clinical disinfectant. It was the secret corner of his world, a room rarely visited by anyone else, not even by Mrs. Phelps.

Kaine was expecting a leading industrialist that afternoon who had lost an eye through cancer. He glanced at his notes, a scribble that only he and his assistant could decipher.

Then he set to work.

The blowing of glass eyes was a dying art, a skill that took many years to perfect — and one he had learnt in Munich. He had spent a full year there as an apprentice to the greatest master of his generation, a Dr. Hubert Rauch. Unlike other oculists — makers of artificial eyes — Kaine preferred to use glass rather than the more usual methyl methacrylate.

The secret of blowing glass eyes was to relax the jaw, and not to rush. Selecting the right pigment mix for the iris, and checking it against his notes, the eye surgeon began the alchemy for which he was internationally known.

Warming the gather, the tiny ball of transparent glass in the burner's flame, he coaxed it, rotating it gently, until it had the consistency of warmed chewing gum. Then, gradually, he teaselled it out, injecting a miniature lance, forcing into it a slow and constant stream of air.

For Amadeus Kaine, the human eye was an organ full of mystery and wonder, and ophthalmology was a science that never ceased to delight. It challenged him to think in new ways, and to break boundaries. The reward was a glorious sense of self-satisfaction — the power to return sight to the blind. But nothing was quite so satisfying as blowing a glass eye, matching the colour perfectly to the original.

As he rested the miniature piece of glass on the cooling rack, Kaine thought of Drusnev, and caught a flash of the supreme leader gorging himself on a bowl of fresh eyes.

He could picture every detail:

The prisoners being marched up from the opal mines in manacles, before being restrained as they were robbed of their sight. He could imagine the tool used for the operation, a kind of simple concave scoop. And he could smell the fear, and hear the commotion — the squishing sound of the scoop, the shouts of the jailers, and the howls of agony.

When the glass eye was ready, Kaine took off his lab coat and paced through into his office. He took in the portrait of George III and a smaller one of Queen Victoria as he walked over to his desk. He logged on and googled the words CANNIBALISM EYE.

Hundreds of results flashed up, most of them detailing the attack on a Miami homeless man who had had part of his face chewed off and swallowed by a man in Dade County. Even for Kaine, a trained surgeon, the photographs of the injury were shocking.

A little further research revealed that cannibalism was nothing new. Throughout history it had provided conquering armies with protein and with an ultimate sense of supremacy. Crusading Knights of the Cross, he learned, would frequently dine on curried hand of Saracen, and Aztecs would think nothing of cooking up their defeated foes. The business of cannibalism appeared to have existed, and even thrived, in almost all societies at one time or another. Its taboo status was certainly a relatively new prohibition, something Kaine found a little bizarre.

The online news archives were packed with cases of unsuspecting foreigners being served human meat while visiting Africa or the Pacific. But there was no word on the ritualistic removal and consumption of eyes. There wasn't even a mention of Bhochnivia's supreme leader and his curious fixation for the little pastries.

Kaine kept on trawling and, eventually, he came across a short article from 1895 describing how a family of Baptist missionaries from Mobile, Alabama, had been attacked and then cooked up in the Kivu region of the Belgian Congo. The only survivor was a young woman by the name of Melanie. She had been unconscious with a fever when the rest of her family had been slaughtered. For some reason, the tribe had spared her life. And, as she regained her strength, they fed her a delicious stew, insisting that she feast on as much as she could eat.

Each night before she slept, the chief would come to her bedside and pop little grape-like fruits into her mouth. Melanie had remarked how utterly delectable they were, and how she had longed for them ever since.

Whenever she asked after her family, the young woman was informed by the tribal elders that they had gone to the next village, but was assured that they would be back soon. They never did return. And, with time, Melanie came to know she had devoured not only her parents, but her brothers, her niece, and her little sister as well.

Having made her escape, and retraced her way back to America, she revealed her story to the horror and fascination of all. Lampooned and shunned, she eventually went mad.

In her delirium, she was chained to an iron bedstead and fed with pig's eyes. She would swallow a dozen a day.

They were the only food she could bear to eat.

Twelve

WARMING THE GLASS eye in his hand, Dr. Kaine rubbed it clean with a sterile medical wipe and pushed it into the ocular socket. The industrialist, a man named Hank Wolfson, blinked a few times, then looked at himself in a hand mirror.

'A perfect match,' he said.

'I do my best,' said the surgeon with a smile.

Wolfson looked down at the desk, where the gold-plated orb was sitting in its stand.

'It's from Bhochnivia, isn't it?' he said.

'Indeed it is. I was just there.'

'I have one too. What did you think of Drusnev?'

Kaine glanced out of the window.

'An unusual man,' he replied.

'He's a nutcase,' said Wolfson, peering into the mirror again. 'Did he feed you any of his special pastries?'

The surgeon turned to face his client, his expression grave.

'Did *you* try one?' he whispered.

'Yes, I did. What about you?'

Kaine moved his head up and down a fraction — more of a tremble than a nod.

'Tasty, wasn't it?'

'Yes. And…'

'And it made you feel twenty years younger?'

'That's right. But why?'

'You're the ophthalmologist, you tell me,' Wolfson said.

Thirteen

THE NEXT WEEK, *Time* ran a three-page feature on Amadeus Kaine, hailing him as the leading eye surgeon of his age. 'He is a man who's on first-name terms with presidents and royalty,' it gushed, 'a man whose surgical skills are unmatched.'

The reporter singled out the way Kaine had donated his time to operate for charities in disaster zones. And he went on to describe the half-dozen ground-breaking procedures he had invented, and the surgical techniques that bore his name.

In the wake of the article, a slew of calls came in from people all over the world, each of them desperate for Dr. Kaine's urgent attention and his services. They included governments and teaching hospitals, charities, VIPs and ordinary members of society.

Mrs. Phelps did her best to field the onslaught of enquiries, but there were so many that she was quickly overwhelmed.

'Tell them I'm dead,' Kaine said with a laugh, 'and perhaps they'll go on and bother someone else. Oh, and Mrs. Phelps, can you please ask the ABSA to take that damned case out of here? They were supposed to take it back weeks ago after the business in Guam.'

Mrs. Phelps looked up. She seemed confused.

'The ABSA, doctor?'

'The American Biological Safety Association. They lent me the biohazard suit, don't you remember?'

The elderly assistant went over to the aluminium case in the corner of the reception. It had been there for so long that Mrs. Phelps regarded it as a piece of the furniture.

'I'll call them right away,' she said.

Fourteen

THE OFFERS OF work kept coming for weeks.

And the more that arrived, the more Dr. Kaine began to wish he could crawl under a rock and hide. He thought of taking a sabbatical, or of writing another book. But, as Mrs.

Phelps often reminded him, now that he was a celebrity in his own right, the public owned a little piece of his soul.

The only comfort was the dining club.

In its company the surgeon indulged himself, revelling in his passion for obscure gastronomy. He would long for the first Tuesday of the month, counting down the days, and then the hours. Secretly, he wished he could tell its members the truth about the curious pastries he had sampled on his visit to Bhochnivia, but the taboo was so great he felt sure that even the seasoned gastronomes of his beloved fraternity would disapprove.

In the weeks since journeying to Vladimir Drusnev's pleasure dome, Kaine had become increasingly fixated with the notion of ocular cannibalism. He knew it was depraved yet, at the same time, he was fascinated by the apparent effect the human eye had had on his body and his mind.

For a full month after eating the pastries, he had felt like a new man. His hair had grown through thick and black. His skin was rosy pink, and his back pain was entirely gone. But best of all was the transformation in mental capability.

The surgeon found that he could do almost any mathematical calculation in his head. He could write poetry too, and consider the most complex intellectual arguments from numerous angles. He managed to pick up basic Mandarin by studying an hour a day, and he mastered the violin as well.

Then, one morning, he awoke to find his skin a tired and sullen shade of grey. His bald patch had returned in the night, and his back was aching terribly. Over breakfast, he struggled to complete a single clue in the *New York Times* crossword. The day before he had finished the entire exercise in ten minutes flat.

It was as though an invisible switch had been turned off on the back of his head. And, rather than being his old self again, he was half the man he had been before eating the supreme leader's pies.

All that morning the usual stream of VIP clients came and went, with Kaine doing his best to accommodate them. He scheduled surgeries for some, examined others, and whispered reassurance to yet more.

But his mind was far away in the Central Asian capital of Moslok.

Worst of all was the craving — the desperate, unhinged craving for the pastries. All he could think of was how to get more.

He considered calling Drusnev's chief of staff to ask for a batch to be sent through the diplomatic bag, or even for a follow-up trip to Bhochnivia. After all, the invitation to go prisoner-hunting had been an open one.

That evening, Amadeus Kaine stayed at work a little later than he had planned, finishing a medical paper for a learned journal. The essay assessed a question of ethics in ophthalmology, a subject that the initial effect of the pastries would have made far easier to debate.

After struggling for a good long while, the surgeon stood up, leaned back on the desk, and picked up the gold-plated orb. Weighing it in his hand, he decided then and there that a little prisoner-hunting was the only solution.

He would call Drusnev's office first thing in the morning.

Fifteen

THAT NIGHT KAINE dreamt of his ex-wife, Francine, the one woman in the world who had the ability to make his blood boil. He dreamed that she was on a chain gang deep in the opal mines. And he dreamed that her hazel eyes were plucked out and stuffed into pastries for Drusnev's table.

The nightmare woke Kaine.

In a cold sweat he reached for his glass of water in the darkness and wondered whether he should see a therapist.

Clambering out of bed, he went online and checked the news. Reading world events did wonders in taking his mind off the ins and outs of his life.

The lead story carried a grotesque picture of a headless body. Drenched in blood, it was missing its hands and feet as well. The corpse was labelled with an attention-grabbing headline:

'MAD DOG' DRUSNEV SLAIN IN MIDNIGHT ATTACK

The story explained how the supreme leader's impoverished people had risen up against him. Hundreds had been slaughtered, most of them members of Drusnev's own family. Realizing that the odds were overwhelming against them, the army had joined the mob and turned their weapons on the misguided aristocracy.

Within hours, Drusnev was captured and killed. His body was dragged through the streets and then decapitated, its eyes apparently swallowed by an onlooker in the crowd.

Kaine clicked on the link to find a gallery of images of Moslok in turmoil, and in jubilation. There were pictures of the presidential palace being looted, of a Rolls-Royce ablaze, of droves of blind prisoners being led up from the opal mines, and of people dancing in the streets.

Damn it, the surgeon thought to himself, I'll never get any of the pastries now.

Sixteen

A FEW DAYS passed, and Kaine excised the right eye of a Canadian billionaire. The procedure was carried out using a piece of equipment that he himself had designed and patented, known as the Kaine Excisor. It consisted of a pair of elliptical blades and a kind of ventouse suction device. The apparatus had been regarded as a revolution in its own right, so much so that every eye surgeon worth their salt now used one.

When the operation was over, the patient was wheeled through to post-op, and the surgical team waited to be dismissed. Dr. Kaine thanked them. He was about to leave, when he noticed the excised eye looking up at him from a kidney dish.

There was something irresistible about it.

'Is that bound for the incinerator?' he asked one of the nurses casually, his mouth watering.

'Yes, doctor.'

'I'd like to make an analysis of this one. I'll send a rundown of what I need. Keep it on ice.'

'Very good, Dr. Kaine.'

Seventeen

THREE DAYS WENT by and the analysis arrived. The surgeon had it sent to his office, where Mrs. Phelps brought it in with his morning coffee and a copy of the *Wall Street Journal*.

'There's a piece about you on page twelve,' she said.

Kaine waved the newspaper away. Opening the envelope, he squinted at the figures.

'Oh,' he said softly. 'Now *that* is interesting. Who would have thought?'

The receptionist was hovering.

'Something unusual, doctor?'

'It must be due to the amino acid content of the melanin, an associated effect of the tyrosine. I'm certain of it.'

'Certain of what, doctor?'

'The taste.'

Mrs. Phelps frowned hard.

'Excuse me?'

Kaine looked up. He had been lost in his own world and was half imagining he was talking to himself.

'Um, er, nothing,' he said, faltering. 'Nothing of importance anyhow.'

The receptionist sauntered back to her position, and when she was gone Kaine looked up the effect of tyrosine on the human sense of taste. That was it, surely. The human eye contains complex arrangements of amino acids, and tyrosine has a profound effect on the metabolism and on neurotransmission in the brain.

Staring out of the window, Amadeus Kaine watched the commuters hurrying in to work. He pitied them for living wasted lives stripped bare of uproar, the kind that visited him on a regular basis.

Stirring his coffee six times to the right, and then to the left, he began to think about the taste again. That taste — succulent, well rounded, and so utterly taboo. It was like nothing he had ever experienced before, as perfect as its consistency, and made all the more appealing by the thought it was the ultimate forbidden fruit.

Stepping over to the mantel, the surgeon checked the time on the Jaeger Atmos clock, his most prized object. He had bought it in an antique shop in Vilnius fifteen years previously.

It was eleven minutes past nine.

Kaine checked the time against his wristwatch, then walked through to where Mrs. Phelps was sitting at the reception desk.

'What time is my next appointment?'

'Not until eleven-fifteen.'

'Who is it?'

'The Ambassador of Hungary. He's come up from DC especially.'

'OK. I'm just running out. But I'll be back in time for him.'

The doctor hurried downstairs and hailed a cab.

'72nd and Broadway.'

The driver didn't answer. He sped off fast, and was soon cruising through Central Park.

Kaine looked out at the face of winter in the trees — the bleak austerity and the cold. It reminded him of Moslok, and that reminded him of Drusnev and the banquet, a memory that reminded him of the eyes.

Everything reminded him of the eyes.

The more he thought of them, the more he craved them. He couldn't work out what he yearned for more — the texture or the taste. They were yin and yang, two inseparable halves of the whole.

The perfect food.

The despised — and now deposed — supreme leader had, without realizing it, happened upon the food of the gods.

The cab rumbled over Central Park West and down 72nd Street. Kaine's gaze jarred from building to building, but he wasn't seeing anything at all. He was thinking — thinking about the genius of Drusnev.

The one man who had understood the passion.

The taste. The craving.

The taxi crossed Broadway and began to slow.

'Which number?' yelled the driver.

'245... that one there... with the green awning.'

Kaine fumbled for change, then jumped out onto the kerb. He closed his eyes, breathed in gently, savouring the patch of street where his youth had been played out. He knew every inch of pavement. Well, he knew every inch of

47

how it had been. It was all gentrified now, awash with glass-fronted emporiums and name-brand stores.

The only one left from the old days was at 245 — Bill's Butchery.

Amadeus Kaine blinked and cleared his throat. A moment later he was inside.

Bill's was an institution, a fourth-generation family business. It had been founded in the twenties by William McMarsh, an immigrant from the Scottish Highlands. His son, grandson, and now great-grandson had all borne the same name in a firm that prided itself on tradition.

Those who patronized Bill's Butchery could rest assured that the customer was always put first. But, most important to the discerning clientele was the fact that successive generations of the McMarsh family made every effort to source exotic meat.

And exotic meat had always been the name of the game at Bill's.

Every scrap of wall space hung with trophies, a kind of gruesome 3D catalogue of what was available.

There were camels' heads and those of crocodiles and kangaroos, gemsbok and zebra, wildebeest and kudu. And, for regular clients, or those in the know, there was the Black Book.

The book was kept behind the counter and its pages contained a cornucopia of wildlife that had at times been sourced for special clients. The inventory included everything from the big cats of the African savannah to the exotic birds and reptiles of the Mato Grosso plateau.

As soon as he saw Kaine step over the threshold, William McMarsh IV lurched up from his stool. He swept round from behind the counter and gave the eye surgeon a rib-crushing hug.

A giant, round-shouldered hulk of a man, he had a tangled grey ZZ Top beard, and a voice so gravelly that it was near impossible to make sense of anything he said. He and Kaine had been childhood buddies. They had grown up together, running errands up and down the West Side.

The surgeon massaged his hands together once the pleasantries were over.

'I'm doing some tests,' he said, 'and need some animal products. One or two things from the Black Book.'

Bill took it from the drawer under the counter and handed it over. It was an inch thick, more of a folder than a book.

The doctor flicked through with concentration.

'They're ophthalmological tests,' he said absently, 'so what I'm after are some eyes.'

'That shouldn't be a problem. It'll take a few days though, depending on what you're after.'

Kaine looked up from the book.

'I need as wide a range as possible.'

'What are we talking about?'

'Some big game, and some more standard stuff.' He sniffed, pinched the end of his nose. 'I'll make you a wish list,' he said, 'and you see what you can get.'

Bill McMarsh teaselled a hand down through his beard.

'Since they're for experimentation I'm assuming they can be, you know... a few days old?'

Kaine's face seemed to tense. He wagged a finger in the direction of his old friend.

'No, no, it's absolutely imperative that they're completely fresh,' he said.

Eighteen

TWO DAYS PASSED and there was still no word from Bill's Butchery, and so Kaine asked Mrs. Phelps to check up on the order.

'He says he needs another week, and that your list is the challenge of his life.'

The surgeon didn't reply. He simply leaned back in his chair and re-enacted the Central Asian banquet in his mind. Amadeus Kaine had never taken drugs in his life, and had never even been tempted. But, for the first time, he understood the anguish of the serious user. The worst thing was the social condemnation of it all, the sense of being an outcast for craving something so proscribed. Then again, as he reasoned it, drug addicts had it easy. They could find a dealer on any street corner ready and willing to supply them the hit.

All of a sudden the telephone rang.

It wasn't the black one that Mrs. Phelps called on, but the red one — reserved for VIP clients. Kaine let it ring six times. Always best to make them think you're busy.

He picked up.

'Hello?'

'Is that Dr. Amadeus Kaine?' asked a thickly accented voice.

'Yes it is.'

'I am Obunda Malinku of the People's Republic of Tenin.'

Kaine racked his memory but couldn't place the country. He typed it quickly into Wikipedia, and found it nestling to the west of the Congo.

The People's Republic of Tenin.
Capital city: Bayotville.
National population: 1,247,000.
Currency: Tenin Dollar.
Language: English and tribal dialects.

'Good afternoon to you, sir. How may I be of assistance?'

There was a muffled screaming sound, as though someone of high authority was extremely displeased. The line went dead. Kaine hung up. He rolled his eyes. Then, after a long pause, the phone rang again.

'Hello?'

'I am sorry,' said the voice. 'There are some communication difficulties.'

'Don't worry about it.'

'I am calling you on behalf of the prime minister's office,' the accented voice explained.

'I see.'

The voice chuckled.

'Well, Mr. Julius Marimba does not!'

'*Julius...?*'

'Marimba... our prime minister.'

'And what exactly is the matter with Mr. Marimba?'

'Hello?'

'I said what is his condition?'

'He has been shot.'

'Where?'

'In the right eye.'

Kaine winced.

'Has an eye surgeon examined him?'

'Yes, sir. I mean no, sir.'

'Well, you need to get a doctor to send me a report. Is that possible?'

The line went dead and Kaine got on with his work. Then, an hour later, the red telephone rang again.

'This is General Oscar Omamba, Chief of Armed Forces in the Republic Tenin!'

'Good afternoon.'

'I hear you are the best eye surgeon in the world.'

'I don't know about that,' Dr. Kaine replied modestly.

'A bullet has pierced the right eye of our prime minister. We need you to come at once.'

Kaine may have pitied the Madison Avenue commuters, but there were times he wished he was one of them.

'I need to speak to a surgeon,' he said, repeating himself.

General Omamba's voice seemed to rise in pitch.

'We are in a challenging position,' he said. 'We are fighting insurgents.'

'Listen, General, I don't want to seem uncharitable, but neither I nor any other surgeon I know is likely to come to a hostile situation. Can you not have the prime minister moved? Could you bring him to New York?'

There was the sound of a desk being thumped with a fist, followed by more shouting.

Another voice came on.

'Dr. Kaine? This is Obunda Malinku. I called you before.'

'Yes, Mr. Malinku.'

'Dr. Kaine, the prime minister is not going to leave. His feet must remain on Tenin's soil. Sir, we are willing to pay you for your services. You can name your price!'

'I can't promise that I shall be able to do anything at all,' Kaine replied. 'The eye has most likely been totally destroyed, and possibly large portions of the brain as well. Is the prime minister conscious?'

'Yes, sir.'

'Well, that's a miracle in itself.'

'What surgical set up do you have there?'

'*Surgical?*'

'Do you have a hospital?'

'Yes, there is a hospital, sir.'

'Are there flights between New York and Tenin?'

Obunda Malinku cleared his throat.

'An aeroplane just left, sir. It will reach New York by nightfall.'

Kaine stood up. He looked hard at the portrait of George III, his eyes counting the buttons on the monarch's coat.

'I shall come for forty-eight hours, and not a moment longer. Do you understand?'

'Yes, sir.'

'And even then, I am coming to make an examination and nothing more.' He paused, clicked his neck. 'As for my fee... I am sure we can work something out.'

Nineteen

THERE WAS NO Champagne or caviar on board the Challenger 601. There weren't even peanuts. The jet was almost twenty years old and had seen much better days. The seat stuffing was coming out, and there were what looked like large bloodstains on the floor of the galley.

'We are borrowing it,' said the pilot awkwardly, as Kaine boarded that night. 'From another African government.'

'Hasn't Tenin got its own aircraft?'

'It had one, but it was destroyed last week in the uprising.'

Kaine had sat down in his seat and thought twice about fastening the buckle.

'*Uprising*?' he whispered.

The pilot shrugged.

'Insurgents. You know. They're all over Africa these days.'

'Is there fighting?'

'Nothing to worry about. It's all over now.'

'Are you sure?'

The pilot didn't answer. He slipped into the cockpit and locked the door firmly behind him.

Nine hours later, bright African sunlight was streaming in through the windows. Despite the lack of refreshments, Kaine had slept well. He finished reading a novel on his Kindle, and then half wondered why he was bothering with Tenin at all.

The answer was that there was something about Africa, something deviously magical, something alluring. The Dark

Continent was in his blood, and it touched him like nowhere else on Earth.

The Challenger jet banked steeply to the right and started to descend fast through the pale blue sky. The pilot announced that landing would be in five minutes. They were still tremendously high. But suddenly, in nothing short of a nosedive, the jet hurtled to the ground.

It tailed off in the nick of time.

Once on the ground, they taxied past the terminal building towards a ramshackle old Nissen hut. All around the airport there was dense, luxuriant vegetation. And there was smoke, too. At first Kaine had assumed it was mist. But as soon as the door was opened, he could smell it. There was a tang of sulphur about it, as though a large stockpile of ordnance had gone up.

As soon as the steps were folded down, three men ran out from the Nissen hut. Two of them were in military fatigues and were armed with Chinese machine guns. The third was dressed in a business suit. He seemed alarmed, his face and clothing drenched with perspiration.

'Welcome to Tenin, Dr. Kaine,' he said. 'I am Obunda Malinku. We spoke on the telephone.'

The surgeon was about to ask something, when Malinku held up a hand.

'There's no time to talk now,' he said urgently. 'The insurgents are closing in on the airport. We must get away.'

They clambered into an old Land Rover with Kaine's voluminous luggage piled in the back, where there was an M60 machine gun mounted. The vehicle was badly damaged and appeared to have caught fire in the recent past.

'Shall we go straight to the hospital?' asked the American. Malinku shook his head.

'It was hit last night. So we will go to the palace. The prime minister is resting there.'

'What treatment has he received?'

'Valium.'

'Is that all?'

Malinku's reply was drowned out by a huge explosion in the near distance. It rocked the ground like an earthquake, and was followed by a second blast, and then a third. The driver accelerated down the rutted dirt road in the direction of the explosions.

'Is it wise to go this way?' Kaine shouted.

'It's the only road,' Malinku replied, climbing into the back to man the M60.

The jungle foliage gave way to shanties and then to low-rise buildings as they approached the outskirts of Bayotville. The air stank of more sulphurous smoke and burning oil. There were too many burnt-out cars and buildings to count.

As for people, there were plenty of dead, peppered all over the ground — men, women, children. The only live people were the soldiers manning the endless checkpoints. At each one they waved the Land Rover quickly through.

From time to time small arms fire rang out. Malinku released the M60's safety catch and returned fire in short, steady bursts.

Clutching the handrail, Kaine was white-knuckled and terrified. There was nothing he disliked more than weaponry or warfare. His blood was so charged with adrenalin that he could have taken a bullet in the ribs and hardly known it.

He got a flash of Drusnev's headless body being pulled through the streets. What if the prime minister was overthrown while he was there? That's all it would take for him to be hacked into mincemeat along with an entire rotten regime. The only difference between him and everyone else was that he couldn't even pronounce the prime minister's name.

A series of extra-large defence barriers came and went, each of them armed more heavily than the last. At the final one the sandbags were stacked four deep, and were finished off with electrified razor-wire and double machine-gun posts.

The Land Rover was waved through fast.

After crossing an open stretch of ground, the vehicle screeched to a halt outside the palace. The American was hurried inside, where General Omamba was awaiting him.

'Thank you for coming to Tenin, Dr. Kaine,' he said in a grave voice. 'I am sorry that the circumstances are not more favourable. If it is any consolation, we have this morning captured the rebel commander.'

'Would you take me to the prime minister?' said the surgeon.

'At once.'

Twenty

EVEN ON THE scale of unscrupulous African dictatorships, the palace was colossal. It boasted three hundred and nine bedrooms, six ballrooms, fifteen kitchens, and its own cathedral. The water in the Olympic-sized swimming pool was imported from the source at Evian, and the walls of every room were overlaid with sheets of twenty-four carat gold.

Amadeus Kaine might more normally have made an effort to show interest in the furnishings, but the fact that the insurgents were closing in disturbed his attention.

Outside, the sound of mortar fire was growing louder and more thunderous, the intervals between the explosions shorter and shorter still. From time to time there was the agonizing wail of a man who had had his legs blown off, or his stomach riddled with lead.

The eye surgeon quickened his pace from a fast walk to a jog, and then to a sprint. As if in a nightmare, the more ground he covered, the further there was to go. Just as he was giving up hope, the general thrust an arm towards a grand doorway.

They entered, zigzagged through a cluster of anterooms, and emerged in a vast bedroom. Octagonal in shape, it had a domed ceiling which could slide away with the flick of a switch. The floor was made from a single sheet of optical-quality glass, allowing a view straight through into a giant aquarium below.

In the middle of the room, the prime minister was lying in a great golden bedstead, fashioned in the shape of a huge brooding eagle. He was propped up, his head copiously bandaged. A drip had been fitted into the leader's arm. Remarkably he was conscious, although in a dreamlike state, a result of the Valium.

Stepping forward calmly, Dr. Kaine introduced himself. He asked for his equipment, and for everyone but the general to leave. Experience had taught him that there was nothing quite so wretched as having hangers-on loitering during an examination, especially one in testing conditions.

On his instructions, the lighting was turned up and the air conditioning was set to super-cool. Having taken a moment to change into sterile clothing and to scrub up, he removed the bandages from the prime minister's head.

The bullet had penetrated at an angle, grazing the nose and entering the middle of the right ocular cavity. Fortunately, it had hit the target when almost spent of energy. Were it to have collided with bone, it would probably have left nothing but a bruise. It seemed as though the bullet, a 9 mm round, had entered the prefrontal cortex, where it was now lodged.

There was no question of the patient ever seeing again through the injured eye, or of the bullet being removed without a full team of specialists.

Kaine stepped away from the bed and beckoned the general to join him.

'The good news is that, with the right treatment, the prime minister will live,' he said. 'But left here, he will die.'

'He cannot leave Tenin!' the general stammered. 'If he does so, our country is lost.'

The surgeon leaned forwards conspiratorially.

'You said, did you not, that you have taken the insurgents' commander alive?'

'Yes, we have. He's in the jail below this palace.'

'I am not a military man,' said Kaine, 'but I have a suggestion.'

'I am listening,' replied General Omamba.

'You could put a sack over the prime minister's head, pretend he's the rebel commander, and send him back to New York with me. He'll get the best treatment there — I'll make sure of it. The insurgents' morale will falter because they'll believe their leader has been taken away. And, when he has recovered a little, the prime minister can make a triumphant return.'

The general held a hand to his chin.

'It sounds as though you have experience of similar situations,' he said.

'I've been around,' replied Kaine. 'You know how it is.'

The prime minister was made ready for the journey, and a sackcloth hood was brought from the jail below. Kaine gave him 300 mg of Valium.

There was the sound of heavy gunfire in the immediate vicinity. Then an explosion. It was so strong that the windows were blown in.

The general brushed the glass off his uniform.

'We must move into a more secure area,' he said, as the prime minister was transferred into a wheelchair.

Again, Kaine found himself jogging down a great corridor, the chandeliers swinging from the continuing barrage of explosions. His face taut, the general led him down to the vault at breakneck speed. The armoured subterranean chamber doubled as a wine cellar.

Inside lay many thousands of bottles of 1er Cru Beaune, Saint-Émilion and Margaux. An entire anteroom was devoted to Champagne, most of it Louis Roederer Cristal. The only exception were thirty bottles of the 1907 vintage Heidsieck, destined for Tsar Nicholas II and recovered from the depths of the Baltic Sea after a German U-boat attack.

Taking refuge in the vault, Kaine wondered why Tenin had no air force to mount an aerial attack on rebel positions. As he pondered it, there was the deafening sound of rotor blades. A Puma helicopter roared above the palace, raining fire on the insurgents.

Within half a minute there were dozens of dead. Their bodies were scattered around the palace complex, mangled by the high-intensity assault.

The general gave a thumbs up.

'That's what we needed,' he said.

'Shall we go now?' the eye surgeon asked.

'It's better to wait until darkness. You'll be taken to the airport by helicopter.'

The soldier popped the cork on a bottle of Cristal and passed it around.

'I suppose this is a good time to ask about your fee,' he said.

Kaine took a swig, wiping the bubbles from his mouth.

'There's something I'd rather have in place of money,' he replied. 'Something hard to get back home in New York.'

'Diamonds?' said the general with a smile. 'We have sacks of them down here.'

'No, not diamonds. Something a little more unusual.'

Twenty-one

JFK HAD NEVER seemed so sweet as it did on the night that the old Challenger 601 landed in dense fog on runway 4L.

Prime Minister Marimba had slept most of the flight. He lay outstretched on the floor, his breathing shallow, and his clothing drenched with sweat. Midway over the Atlantic, Kaine had administered another shot of Valium. Then, as the aircraft began the descent, he checked the leader's vital signs and whispered words of encouragement.

'We're nearly there now. Just a little longer and you'll be living it up at Mount Sinai.'

As for himself, Kaine had never felt better. He was floating on cloud nine, his senses buzzing through a kind of primitive alchemy. Throughout college his friends had taunted him to try drugs — but who needed drugs when you could knock back a dozen or two human eyes?

The effect was immediate and far more profound.

General Omamba had thought nothing odd about the surgeon's request. Fulfilling it had been far easier and cheaper than making a wire transfer from a Swiss bank, or even packing up a bag of precious gems.

At dusk he had sent a couple of his men out into the darkness beyond the palace. They were given instructions on what to do, and ordered to use their bayonets with care.

Only one of the conscripts had returned.

The other had been shot through the head by a sniper lying low in what was until recently the Café Royale. The soldier who survived had filled his helmet with fresh eyes. There must have been forty of them, a harvest from twenty dead insurgents. Surprisingly, there was very little blood. Rather like a child's illustration of a strange creature from the deep, they were disturbing but utterly fascinating. Kaine couldn't take his own eyes off them.

'That was fast,' he had said. 'How many did you get?'

'Plenty,' mumbled the conscript.

'Good work,' replied the general, taking a long swig of Cristal. 'Go and find a box and we'll wrap them up.'

Twenty-two

ON THE RETURN flight, the doctor had waited for the Challenger to climb to cruising altitude and for the crackle of gunfire to subside. Then he had switched on his seat's lamp and, a little cautiously, had picked up the box. It was sitting on the coffee table.

Untying the string, he'd pulled away the lid. What touched him first was the smell. It was difficult to describe — metallic, oleaginous, and succulent. Even before his mind had made sense of the eyes, his mouth was salivating.

Amadeus Kaine had unbuckled his seatbelt and walked back to the galley. He'd pulled open one or two drawers and found a silver-plated soup spoon and a crystal salt-shaker. Back in his seat, he had put the box on his lap. Without any apprehension he had begun shovelling the eyes into his mouth.

Whereas President Drusnev's pastries had contained cooked eyes, the ones from the urban battlefield of Bayotville had been raw and extremely fresh.

As soon as the first one had touched his tongue, Kaine had realized that although remarkable at the time, the supreme leader's delicacies paled in comparison with the real thing.

And the real thing was raw, stripped bare of pastry and seasoning. Its texture was similar in softness to a well-cooked poached egg. But unlike the egg, there was a variety in consistency. The cornea was a little tougher than the back of the eye, and the muscles on the sides more meaty than the rest.

As for the taste, it was not dissimilar to *marron glacé*, with a hint of *maguro* sushi thrown in. The more Kaine devoured, the more he had begun to appreciate the subtleties between one eye and the next. Some were a little more astringent on the back of the throat, as if somehow unripe, while others melted in the mouth, their juices disgorging themselves like the finest Beluga caviar.

By the time the aircraft landed at JFK, the surgeon was digesting the meal. He had felt full but not bloated, and had found himself wondering how he could ever stomach what was considered to be normal cuisine again.

But the most remarkable thing was the effect the illicit food was having on him. As before, in Moslok, he could feel the blood pumping in his muscles and the colour returning to his cheeks. His mind was racing, as though he could compute any mental calculation, or discuss an idea of the most intense complexity.

The fresh eyes had not only tasted far more delicious than their Central Asian counterparts, but their effect was more immediate and far more rejuvenating, too.

As he sat back buckled up in the seat, the doctor could actually feel his bald patch growing over and his back pain easing once again. The sensation would have astounded any medical man, but it was all the more amazing to Kaine, who had devoted his professional life to the study of the very organ that effected this change.

Twenty-three

At JFK, an ambulance met the private jet.

An hour and a half after landing, Amadeus Kaine began the complex operation to remove the bullet from behind the prime minister's eye. A surgical staff of fifteen assisted in a procedure that took six hours.

When it was over, Kaine took a cab home to his apartment and locked himself away. He left a message for Mrs. Phelps, asking her to cancel all his appointments, and to inform anyone enquiring that he was unwell.

The truth was quite the opposite.

It was as though the world outside was too lethargic, too languid, that it couldn't keep up. With each hour that passed, Kaine felt stronger and more mentally agile, until every fibre was vibrating with electrical energy. Never in his life had he felt so vital, so astonishingly spirited and alive.

On the first day he wrote an entire symphony. After that he dedicated himself to considering world hunger. He created a blueprint for a new kind of society — one that was truly fair but without the glaring pitfalls of communism. The next day he devoted himself to writing a five-hundred-page masterwork. Entitled *Eye Spy: A Surgeon's Vision*, it was a cultural consideration of sight from prehistory to the present. The day after that, he designed a machine to create free plentiful energy from seawater.

On the fourth day, Kaine returned to work.

Mrs. Phelps offered consolation at his illness. The eye surgeon shooed her away. He looked through his mail and asked if there was anything that couldn't wait.

Touching a finger to a name on her memorandum pad, the elderly assistant said:

'This gentleman keeps calling.'

'Who does?'

'This journalist from the *LA Times*.'

'What does he want?'

'A comment on the outbreak of oculosis.'

Amadeus Kaine tossed the pile of mail he was holding onto the desk.

'Where is it — the outbreak?' he asked quickly.

'Up in Maine. It's been headline news for a week.'

Striding over to his laptop, Kaine punched up the story.

'Just what I predicted!' he exclaimed.

Twenty-four

THE NEXT MORNING, Bill's Butchery delivered.

The eyes were packed in polystyrene, cooled with crushed ice and were labelled — URGENT.

Mrs. Phelps took the delivery and assumed the doctor was having a dinner party. She brought the sealed package through to the office.

'Where would you like this, doctor?' she asked.

Kaine looked up. His mind was on oculosis, the mystery eye disease that had appeared from nowhere. As soon as he saw the label, he jolted out from his chair.

'Put it in the lab, would you?'

'Yes, doctor.'

Having finished reading the first comprehensive report on the outbreak, he called a fellow surgeon up in Augusta. Then, washing his hands, he slipped back into the lab. Once alone, he bolted the door and cut away the packing tape with a scalpel blade.

Inside the box, the various eyes had been individually wrapped in protective transparent containers. They made for quite a beautiful sight. Bill McMarsh had outdone himself, sourcing the freshest examples and carefully labelling each one.

Before dining, Kaine went to the sink and washed his hands a second time. And then a third. After that, he counted backwards from one hundred in multiples of three. It was at moments of heightened anticipation that his OCD was at its worst.

Calming himself, he applied a moisturizer, and thought back to the days when he would wrestle Bill McMarsh out on the street. He sat down, his movements unhurried and considered.

And then with care he opened the first package.

A miniature label read — *Kangaroo*. Kaine popped its contents into his mouth. It went down smoothly, rather like an oyster. On a notepad he jotted:

Kangaroo: Muscular, congealed. A hint of tobacco and cinnamon.

Next, he opened the package containing a lion's eye — no doubt, he imagined, sourced from the overstocked hunting grounds of San Diego Zoo. It tasted a little saltier than the first, rather more bitter than he liked, with an infusion of nutmeg. The third eye was from a male kudu, the fourth from a crocodile, and the one after that was from a wild boar. Each one was quite different in both consistency and taste — a point that interested the doctor greatly.

By the end of the degustation, he had filled three sheets with notes and had swallowed fifteen eyes. The most delicious had been without doubt the llama's eye, and the oryx had been the worst.

But none of them had been nearly as enjoyable as a human eye.

When he had consumed all the samples that Bill McMarsh had sent over, Amadeus Kaine went back through to the office and sat in his chair. His mind was racing again, and he considered the strange predicament in which he now found himself.

This new and unknown superfood was, as he reasoned it, one that was unlikely to be discovered by anyone else. But the human variety alone had provided the seemingly miraculous effect.

There were plenty of diets rich in melanin, but synthesizing the amino acid content didn't appear to be enough. Kaine tried desperately to think of a trustworthy confidant in the world of medicine with whom to discuss the subject. The last thing he wanted, though, was a lecture on ethics. He knew that consuming human tissue of any kind was regarded as abhorrent, wrong, and would be considered as utterly distasteful by his peers.

Yet, if it had had such an intense and transformative effect on one man, imagine what effect it could have on an entire society. Surely there was a way of creating an analogue, of replicating the effect with human tissue.

Leaning back, Dr. Kaine swivelled around and gazed through the window. Madison Avenue was awash with ant-like figures, as it was on most afternoons.

All those people, Kaine thought to himself. They end up dying, and their eyes go to waste. It's as simple as that. A few may be used in surgery, but not the eyes of the masses, the people who die every day. He rocked back and forth thoughtfully. Surely there was no great harm in sacrificing a few eyes if it meant a brighter future for all?

Twenty-five

THE NEXT DAY was the first Tuesday of the month.

More usually, Kaine would have been beside himself with anticipation and delight. But on this occasion he hadn't given it a moment's thought. Instead of being titillated by the obscure fare, he was rather blasé about it, and even a little bored.

As far as he was concerned, he had discovered the ideal dish. The burning question was whether it had the same effect on everyone else as it did on him.

The dinner that night was to be hosted by Samuel Greenstead, an investment banker with a lisp and a penchant for the high life. He never neglected dropping into the conversation whom he had lunched with that day, or how many zeros there were on the end of the current deal he was chasing. He was stout and meaty, his complexion waxy, and his dress sense eccentric though expensive.

His apartment was one of those sprawling gems in the Dakota Building, with a good view out over Central Park. The décor was impeccable, at least for a banker. As Kaine reasoned it, this was nothing very special, for he had merely got his secretary to hire the most celebrated interior designer in the land.

Over much brut Champagne, the members of the Obscure Cuisine Dining Club chit-chatted before dinner, catching up with the previous month's milestones.

The pilot asked about the outbreak of oculosis up in Augusta.

'It was sure to happen,' said Kaine, taking a sip of dry Austrian Riesling. 'Like bird flu it has mutated, and now it's spreading. It's essentially out in the open — on the wind.'

'How's it caused?' Herbert Hoffman asked.

'By a virus. Pure and simple. It eats away at the iris, destroying the structure of the eye from the inside out.'

'Is there nothing that can be done?'

The doctor sighed.

'I'm working on something,' he said. 'It's radical, and still under wraps, but there's always a chance.'

Greenstead called his guests to the table and toasted the fraternity with an '82 Fixin.

'I am hoping I can excite you with what's to come,' he lisped. 'The bar is set very high, and I have done my utmost to keep it so.'

A butler paced through with a tureen. It was steaming lightly and left a trail of what smelled like charred bacon. A ladle of the contents was poured onto each plate.

'An *amuse-bouche*,' said Greenstead grandly. 'Broiled baby iguana in a béchamel sauce.'

The dish proved popular. The film director and one other asked for more.

Then came the main meal.

The first course was warthog carpaccio, followed by the *pièce de résistance* — grasshoppers stewed in Armagnac. They were eaten, as is ortolan, with a starched linen cloth draped over the head to prevent the vapour from escaping.

Kaine ate his grasshoppers and sensed his pores opening in the steam. The flavour was impressively profuse, with an aftertaste of linseed. He looked up and took in the other members with cloths over their heads. For the first time, the doctor found himself tiring of the club, and he suddenly regretted ever being associated with it at all.

The reason was not so much the food, as the people.

Scooping the last grasshopper onto his fork, and then into his mouth, Kaine decided to conduct a little test. He would bring up the question of cannibalism. If the members applauded it, he would remain in the club. If they rejected it, he would leave and never return.

'I visited a Central Asian republic recently,' he said, as the plates were cleared. 'It was a complete autocracy of course — most of them are — but they have a curious tradition. They eat little pies.'

'What are they made with?' asked the pilot.

'With roasted bats?' Greenstead lisped, laughing out loud.

'Not exactly,' Kaine replied. 'You see, they are filled with human eyes.'

The other members sat there, motionless. One of them, the director, gasped.

'That's awful!'

'It's beyond awful!' exclaimed another.

'It's wicked,' said Greenstead.

'But is it really?' said Kaine.

Herbert Hoffman put his head in his hands.

'What do you mean?' he exclaimed.

Amadeus Kaine took a long sip of Burgundy and swilled it around his mouth pensively.

'I mean that we sit here month after month,' he said, 'eating some of the most peculiar dishes imaginable. Indeed, some of the foods we have sampled bear little resemblance to food at all. But the very thought of eating our own meat is considered repugnant — the last taboo.'

'Amadeus, my dear Amadeus, listen to yourself,' said Greenstead, his voice trembling and his lisp altogether gone.

'Believe me, gentlemen, I have considered it at great length.'

'Did you try them? The pastries... did you eat one?'

'Oh yes. I ate several.'

'How did they taste?'

Again Kaine sipped his wine, delighting in the moment.

'They tasted like nothing I have ever imagined,' he said.

Twenty-six

THREE DAYS AFTER the gourmet dinner, the first case of oculosis struck Massachusetts. The day after that, there was an outbreak in New York, and six cases in Florida. A sense of confused urgency prevailed, and it quickly developed into full-blown panic.

The news channels were awash with experts and politicians spewing conflicting messages in polished sound bites. None of them said anything of real value at all.

Dr. Kaine's telephone rang constantly, but Mrs. Phelps had been given strict instructions to put none of the calls through. The surgeon was lying low in his laboratory, hunched over an electron microscope. Every so often, he checked a page on the internet, or sent a line or two of email, eager for updates on the changing pathology of the disease.

Six months before, during a visit to Guatemala, he had isolated oculosis for the first time. It was prevalent there, and had meted out an extraordinary path of destruction. But the illness had remained insulated back then.

From the first moment he studied it, Kaine's fear had been that oculosis would spread in a grand pandemic, the likes of which the world had not seen since the medieval Black Death.

As far as he was concerned, a major outbreak was inevitable and nothing more than a matter of time.

The energy rush from the Bayotville eyes began to subside. As before, Dr. Kaine sensed his skin sagging, his hair thinning and, worst of all, his mental faculties fading fast. He could feel it coming on, his capabilities dissipating, as though he were enduring a decade's worth of ageing in a few hours.

All he could think of was how to get a fresh supply of eyes.

The Supreme Leader Vladimir Drusnev may have been dead, but thanks to Kaine the Prime Minister of Tenin was recovering in New York's Mount Sinai. As he saw it, he could easily travel back with the recuperating potentate. Thinking of it, there was surely no harm in calling General Omamba and asking for a consignment of eyes to be sent through in the diplomatic bag. It surely wasn't much to ask given that he was credited with having saved the prime minister's life.

First things first though.

Amadeus Kaine had an appointment at the New York Presbyterian Hospital, where a young woman had just been brought in with oculosis. Taking a cab down to 68th Street, he made his way to the Weill Cornell Center, where she was under quarantine.

Department chief Dr. Eugene Faust met him at the reception.

'I'm a huge fan,' he whispered unctuously. 'Just sorry to meet you in such adverse conditions.'

Kaine greeted the praise with a smile and asked for the patient's charts. A nurse hurried up with them.

'Have you had any other cases so far?'

Faust shook his head.

'But there are now cases up and down the Eastern Seaboard. The growth is exponential. And, as you know, there's no treatment… there's absolutely nothing we can do.'

'I'd like to examine the woman, if that's OK.'

'Of course. We have screened her off down the hall.'

Kaine put on scrubs, disinfected his hands, and made his way through. The woman was in her early twenties and had dark auburn hair, and a rather anaemic complexion. She was lying back in a hospital bed, and she seemed anxious, as though the world was locking her out. Her right eye was covered in a bandage.

'I'm Dr. Amadeus Kaine,' the surgeon said, 'and I'm here to help.'

'I'm Emily… Emily Buchanan.'

'Emily, I'd like to examine you,' said Kaine tenderly. 'But first I have a few questions.'

'OK.'

'Can you tell me if you've had any access to farm animals in the last few days?'

'Er... no, not that I can think of.'

'What about household pets... dogs, cats, rabbits... even horses.'

'No. None at all.'

'What about wild animals?'

Emily choked out a laugh.

'I live in the Bronx,' she said. 'There's no wild animals up there except for the hoods.'

Kaine didn't smile at the joke.

'When did you first experience itching in the eye?'

'Three nights ago.'

'And was there a blurring sensation right away?'

'No, that came on the day after. It felt as if I'd been slugged on the back of the head with a baseball bat.'

The eye surgeon peered into the eye with an ophthalmoscope. He strained to stay composed, even though the entire structure of the iris was compromised.

'That's very good,' he said calmly.

'I'm gonna be OK, aren't I?' Emily replied, on the verge of breaking down.

'Of course you are. But right now we need to watch you very carefully. You're in good hands with Dr. Faust.'

Out in the corridor, he filled six pages of his notebook with unreadable scrawl, glancing at Emily's file again and again. When Dr. Faust approached, Kaine scribbled a number on a blank sheet and tore it out.

'This is my cell,' he said. 'It's imperative that you text me right away if any more suspected cases come in. The symptoms of itching, pain at the back of the head, nausea... all the usual stuff.' The doctor drew a short breath. 'One more thing,' he said, 'we need to ascertain whether there's an association between oculosis patients and wildlife.'

'I understand that Emily Buchanan lives in the urban jungle,' said Dr. Faust.

Kaine nodded.

'I know, but we have to isolate how and where the transmission occurred.'

Ten minutes later, the doctor was in a cab heading over to Mount Sinai. He was exhausted, his mind churning as it craved another fix. The need for another batch of human eyes was drowning out everything else. It was senseless and futile, like the hankering of an addict whose grip on reality was lost.

Taking out his cell phone, he called General Omamba. It rang for a long time and the line went dead. Kaine called a second time. On the third ring a young man picked up. He sounded frightened, his voice frail against a deafening background noise.

'General Oscar Omamba passed away an hour ago,' he said. 'And the palace is being stormed.'

The sound of high velocity machine-gun fire and screams followed, after which came a tremendous explosion.

The line went dead.

'Damn it!' Kaine shouted, his face flushing with rage.

The cab driver glanced back in his rear-view mirror.

'Everything all right, sir?'

'Huh?'

'You OK, bud?'

'Yes.'

'Having a bad day, huh? Know what that's like. My wife just walked out on me. Thirty-two years and she picks up and leaves, just like that.'

The eye surgeon stared out of the window at the endless apartment buildings of First Avenue.

'I've changed my mind,' he said suddenly. 'I don't need to go to Mount Sinai any longer. Take me to the Upper East Side.'

Twenty-seven

THAT EVENING THE news networks were dominated by oculosis.

A word that had so recently been unknown was now on every tongue. Fear had turned to panic, and now panic became hysteria, the kind which spreads like wildfire through urban landscapes. Fanned by the mass media, the frenzy took hold in the most debased way.

When out in the streets, ordinary people took to wearing ski goggles. Convenience stores were attacked by thugs claiming to have the disease. They had no need for weapons, because they were armed with the perfect punchline: *Hand over the cash or I'll spit in your eye!*

In Georgia, a train driver was unable to stand the burning sensation any longer. He slammed his commuter train into another, killing fifty-five. And, in Pennsylvania, an entire family was infected. The journalist reporting the story said they had caught it from one another, that in a single day they had all gone blind.

Twenty-eight

DAY AND NIGHT Amadeus Kaine worked away at understanding the virus. He isolated the protein crystallin as a potential key that might unlock the riddle of oculosis.

Cancelling all clients, he laboured around the clock in a desperate attempt to understand the disease's pathology. He spent hours staring into the microscope and scouring the internet for new case studies. The problem was keeping abreast of all the new cases. The virus was morphing so fast that anything but the most recent case study was hopelessly out of date.

For a moment Kaine considered teaming up with the FBI's Emergency Medical Support Program. They called him endlessly, begging for his help. But the doctor had worked with the unit before, and he knew how they tied themselves up with red tape just when they needed to think freely.

Instead, he made use of the data coming to him from ophthalmic contacts across the country. The more he studied, the more he was driven mad by craving and desire.

An eye.

A delicious, succulent, moist human eye.

He could taste it, grinding the luscious tissue between his back teeth, moving it around his mouth, and then slowly swallowing it. The harder he tried to push the thought out of his mind, the more it seemed to creep in, until it was all there was left.

Such was Kaine's reputation that he could have called up any teaching hospital in the nation and asked for samples — with or without the oculosis disease.

But a quick hors d'oeuvre was surely not the solution.

The answer was to use science to understand why human eyes were so palatable, and how they affected the complex synaptic processes in the brain. Achieve that with a workable synthesis and, as he constantly reminded himself, there would be no end to his success.

Twenty-nine

THE DAYS DRAGGED on, as did the surgeon's research, and the hysteria outside. Kaine locked himself away, and even arranged for a bed to be moved into the office. Going home to his apartment was a waste of time, and time was the one element against him. Indeed, anything that got in the way of research was regarded as a waste of time — including shaving, showering, or eating.

Mrs. Phelps grew increasingly worried about her employer. Whenever she came to him with a question, he would scowl, or simply not answer at all. And when she asked him to sign paperwork, or to authorize a payment, he looked at her as though she were mad.

'I don't require your services any longer,' he told her coldly one morning.

'But Dr. Kaine…'

'Thank you, Mrs. Phelps. Please leave me now.'

The surgeon strode back into the lab and closed the door forcefully behind him. The room was awash with papers and discarded samples from abandoned experiments.

After many days there came a point at which the outside world broke through.

Dr. Faust sent a message to report on Emily. Her right eye having gone entirely blind, the left was now experiencing the initial symptoms.

Thrusting his head under a laboratory tap, Amadeus Kaine pushed back his wet hair and shook the water from his hands. Then he put on a clean shirt and a coat, and hurried out to hail a cab.

He was close to a breakthrough. He could feel it. But there still wasn't enough reliable information from which to draw firm conclusions. And information was what it was all about — information and time.

A stickler for minutiae, Kaine would more usually have noticed every detail of the taxi ride. But his focus had narrowed to the slenderest of tunnels.

He closed his eyes.

All he could see was an eye with oculosis, the iris severely damaged. It was sitting on a plate, with his shadow looming over it, a polished silver spoon inching closer.

Thirty

NEW YORK PRESBYTERIAN was being mobbed by members of the public. There were armed guards on the main gates, military-spec goggles tight against their faces. Some were wearing green biohazard suits and had breathing apparatus strapped to their backs.

Dr. Kaine made his way through to the ophthalmic department, where Faust led him down the corridor towards Emily's room.

'We've now got thirty patients in here,' he said. 'God knows how many others have gone down with it across New York, let alone the nation.'

'When did Emily's left eye begin to go?' Kaine asked brusquely.

'This morning. We've sedated her. We had to.'

The eye surgeon went into the darkened room and, as he did so, his energy changed. He was suddenly calm, reassuring and relaxed. He reminded Emily who he was. She recognized his voice at once.

'I'm going to go blind in the other eye now,' she said in a quiet voice, 'aren't I?'

'I hope not,' Kaine replied. 'I know you've probably seen a thousand TV hospital dramas with cheesy scripts,' he said, 'but I need you to trust me. It must sound implausible, but it's the truth.'

'Then you're the only one within a hundred miles of here who's got any hope at all.'

The doctor was going to ask Emily a question about the sensation in the exterior of her eyes when the door opened.

It was Dr. Faust.

'Could I see you outside?' he said quickly.

Excusing himself, Kaine slipped out into the corridor.

'Yes?'

'Sorry to jump in like that, but a trauma victim's just been rushed in.'

'Oculosis?'

'No, no… a guy from a building site with the end of a drill bit in his eye.'

'Who've you got on standby?'

'That's the problem. We're stretched with all the oculosis cases. They're coming in thick and fast.'

Fifteen minutes later, Kaine had cleared the paperwork, made an initial examination, and was scrubbing up. The surgical team all knew of his work and his high-flying reputation. He was glad to be helping out, although he knew very well it was wasting valuable time that could be used refining the theory on oculosis.

The injured workman was wheeled in.

There was no choice but to remove his damaged eye and control the bleeding. The operation went according to plan, and the patient was wheeled through to recovery.

The excised blue eye was still in the theatre, sitting in a kidney dish along with the drill bit. It was partially covered with a lump of bloodied dressing, apparently forgotten in the rush. The anaesthetist and the support staff were nowhere to be seen.

Kaine jerked away the dressing and sensed his mouth watering. He almost choked. The more he looked at it, the more he was overcome with the symptoms of an addict in withdrawal. His pulse was racing, his brow streaming with perspiration, the blood vessels in his cheeks constricting.

Suddenly, without thinking, he picked out the shard of steel and gulped down the eye as though it was a piece of hot ravioli.

He didn't even chew.

The nurse came in.

'I could have sworn the excised tissue was in this dish, doctor,' she said.

'Er, um,' Kaine faltered. 'No, um, I think your colleague took care of it.'

'Oh, thanks.'

She went out and Kaine slipped into a side office. He needed a moment alone, a moment to collect his thoughts and to enjoy the oncoming rush.

It began with a warming of the neck muscles and, by gradual degrees, a kind of tightening at the back of the head. It was difficult to explain, but it felt right. Oh, how it felt right — as if it was somehow connected to the primate in us all.

Leaning back against the desk, Dr. Kaine held on tight as the full force of the euphoria unfolded. He felt elated, yet totally calm, his senses more alert than at any time he could remember, his hands and feet tingling, ready for fight or flight.

It was as though his neural cortex was turned triumphantly on.

All at once his brain was ablaze.

He could feel individual thoughts streaming at lightning speed through the twisted labyrinth of neurons and synapses. He was strapped aboard the neural extravaganza of his life, a slaloming rollercoaster of thoughts. For every question hinted at there were a hundred brilliant answers, generated with an immediacy unthinkable to anyone else alive.

Struggling to focus, Kaine strove desperately to harness the moment, to make the most of the precious stolen eye.

He considered his research into oculosis.

There were two fundamental points — how the virus had been transmitted to humans, and the role of the protein crystallin.

The answers came in a lightning bolt flash.

The disease had mutated from domesticated chickens. There was no question about it. It was being spread to the American population through the nation's factory-like slaughterhouses. Kaine remembered seeing a documentary that prophesied such a disease, in which it was claimed that all the fast-food outlets in the US relied on the same thirteen vast abattoirs.

And what of crystallin?

The surgeon allowed his breathing to calm. He scrolled back through tens of thousands of documents, paper and electronic. Visualizing himself scanning them all, he re-read each one.

Crystallin.

The word kept appearing, but in different contexts. It made no sense. What did a protein in the cornea and lens have to do with the disintegration of the iris?

Kaine concentrated like he had never concentrated before.

Connecting every fragment of knowledge he had ever heard, read, or seen, he cross-referenced in three dimensions.

And slowly, a pattern emerged.

As with the first answer, it was simplicity itself.

The human iris was susceptible to increased levels of crystallin, just as it was sensitive to anything else. But the difference with this specific protein was in the way that it induced a rapid deterioration in the cells when exposed to light.

The solution had to rely on creating a barrier to protect the cornea.

Amadeus Kaine wiped the sweat from his face. It was as though he was baking alive. Ripping off his surgical shirt, he wiped it over his face and panted for a minute and a half like a bloodhound after the chase. Then, straining to compose himself again, he slipped the surgical shirt back on and went out into the corridor.

Dr. Faust strode up.

'There you are, doctor,' he said. 'I was looking for you. Wanted to congratulate you. I hear the surgery went well.'

'It was quite routine.'

'The team is singing your praises.'

'For not saving a man's eye?' Amadeus Kaine shrugged. 'I wish we lived in the future. A realm where unimaginable possibilities await us.'

Thirty-one

FOR THREE DAYS, the eye surgeon worked. He didn't stop for more than five minutes in all that time. It was a race against the clock. The effect of the freshly excised eye would wear off, and he had to squeeze every last fragment of intelligent thought from it first.

Experimenting with a full spectrum of natural light, he determined a range that blocked the effect of crystallin. It lay above the upper end of the UV range, in a scale invisible to the human eye.

Four days later, he emerged from his lab and called the mayor's office, suggesting that a press conference be held. In more normal circumstances it might have seemed a rather theatrical way to behave. But these were anything but normal circumstances.

News that the celebrated ophthalmologist was about to speak spread rapidly through Manhattan, the East Coast, and the nation. With oculosis now infecting almost every community in North America, there was unprecedented media interest from news channels all over the world.

The media had gathered in the ballroom of the Mandarin Oriental, on West 57th Street. With standing room only, the atmosphere was one of high electricity. Satellite trucks were parked bumper to bumper around the block, and reporters from around the globe were doing pieces to camera against the arctic winter wind.

Amadeus Kaine was comfortable with the media. He knew as well as anyone that they were the key to success in his career, just as much as they would now be the key in spreading the word of his initial breakthrough.

On the dot of twelve noon he entered, the mayor of New York beside him. Walking through to the podium with brisk strides, he stepped up to the microphone, tapped a thumb to it twice, and began:

'Ladies and gentlemen,' he said, 'thank you for attending. Some of those watching right now will be familiar with my work. But, I imagine, far more will be familiar with oculosis,' he paused, took a sip of water, and looked out at the sea of heads. 'This is an extreme crisis, one that requires an extreme solution,' he said. 'I'm not claiming that we've got that yet, but I am confident that, given time, we can beat this disease.'

'Time is what we don't have!' a voice called out from the back.

'You're very right. Time is our enemy, not our friend. And that's why I am making available today an initial treatment. Full details will be circulated to the press after this meeting.'

'What's the treatment, Dr. Kaine?' another voice shouted out.

'A combination of brimonidine tartrate eye drops and a filtration lens.'

'Do we yet know how oculosis is being spread?' asked a reporter from CNN.

'Yes,' said Kaine. 'I'm confident that a direct link will be established between the battery farming of poultry and this disease. It explains why the epidemic is being experienced most keenly in the United States, where the industrialization of chicken farming in particular is a national phenomenon.'

'What about those people who have already contracted oculosis, doctor?'

Kaine pinched the bridge of his nose and closed his eyes for a moment.

'I believe that a treatment will be perfected to repair damaged sight,' he said. 'And it's for that reason that I have to go and prepare for the operation.'

A journalist from Fox News waved a hand.

'Can you tell us who your guinea pig is?' she said.

'A young woman, whose sight has been lost in the right eye, and whose left eye is now experiencing the same symptoms.'

'What are your chances of success?'

Dr. Kaine held up his hands.

'I'd say that they're stacked against me succeeding, six to one.'

Thirty-two

THE NEXT MORNING, after the best possible surgical team had been assembled, Emily Buchanan was wheeled into the operating theatre. She had been apprehensive at first but, as she saw it, she was being given a golden lottery ticket — the only one of its kind.

Kaine was not a religious man, agnostic at best. But before stepping into surgery, he prayed. Never in his career had the sight of so many people hinged on one operation.

As he stood there, his eyes closed, his hands clenched together, he sensed his mental faculties diminishing. The effect of the workman's eye had gone. He was on his own and despite it he had to perform a miracle.

There was no way to source another eye. No legal method, at any rate. Steadying his nerves, he scrubbed up, and stepped through into the theatre, reminding himself that he was the best of the best. He was Amadeus Kaine.

Seven hours of surgery followed.

By the time it was over, it was afternoon. The flat winter light streamed in through the hospital windows. But Emily's room was dark, the blackout curtains tightly drawn.

For an entire day the patient was permitted to rest, her eyes copiously bandaged. Outside the hospital, the world's press was camped out, awaiting news of the operation.

A full day after she had been wheeled out of the theatre, Kaine unwrapped Emily's bandages himself, feeling for them in the darkness. The last thing the surgeon wanted was to strain his patient's eyes, and so he refrained from drawing the curtains open or turning on the lights.

Emily was lying in the bed, motionless, like a reclining Buddha, too frightened to breathe.

When the bandages and padding were completely gone, she let out a faint cry.

'I can't see anything,' she said.

'Neither can I,' replied Kaine, 'because we're sitting here in darkness.'

He turned on his cell phone and laid it on the bed.

'Light!' Emily shrieked. 'I can see light!'

The eye surgeon breathed in hard.

'What about now?' he asked, moving the phone close to Emily's face.

'Verizon!' she shouted. 'I can see you use Verizon!'

Thirty-three

THE NEXT EVENING, Kaine appeared on CNN's main news show. He had spent the day conducting tests on Emily's sight, and in publishing details of the operation online for the worldwide ophthalmological community. Although exhausted, and craving another eye, he was elated by the recent success.

Welcoming him to the show, the anchor Casper Wallace gave a firm handshake and a smile.

'Going live now,' he said.

The titles rolled and Kaine was introduced, with Emily Buchanan's treatment being hailed as a glimmer of light in an ocean of darkness.

'The first question I have for you, doctor, is how oculosis could have made the jump from animal to human, and how it could have affected our lives so fast.'

Dressed in a Harris tweed jacket and dark cashmere turtleneck, Amadeus Kaine thought hard before replying.

'We like to imagine that we have nature under our thumbs,' he said after a long pause, 'that we live in a world that's under *our* spell. But nothing could be farther from the truth, and oculosis is a reminder of that. The disease has lain dormant in poultry for centuries, possibly even for millennia, but it's made the leap because of the way we farm. Indeed, I wouldn't call it farming at all — I'd call it industry... industry of the most depraved and unnatural kind.'

'And what of the operation you carried out yesterday?'

'Well, I'm proud to say that my team restored the sight of a brave young woman, a woman who had been affected by the advanced symptoms of oculosis.'

'But what of the thousands of ordinary Americans who have been affected... are they going to have to undergo lengthy and costly operations as well?'

'I hope not — at least in the long term. We are working on a treatment, one that can reverse the symptoms, and I am confident that we will achieve it. But, for now, an operation is the only choice.'

Amadeus Kaine looked across at Wallace, his eyes locking onto the talk-show host's freckled face. Taking in his sapphire-blue eyes, he imagined them in his mouth. He could taste them, feel them between his cheek and his tongue, and sensed them being crushed by his back teeth.

Wallace asked another question, but Kaine didn't hear. The doctor was in his own world, a world where human eyes provided a rare gastronomy and opened the doors to a society of astonishing intellectual promise.

'Excuse me, Casper,' he said awkwardly, 'could you repeat your question?'

'Yes of course. I was merely asking whether you had ever imagined that a disease such as oculosis would strike as it has done?'

'I've imagined it night after night for decades,' he said, his voice suddenly touched with anger. 'And any sensible American ought to have been doing the same. We limit our spectrum of food to a handful of meats and other products, each of them reduced to the most pitiful grade. Ask yourself why in the US we have been hit with oculosis while the rest of the world has so far escaped! The answer is the wholesale industrialization of food.'

There was the glint of a smile in Wallace's eye, a glint that caused Kaine to salivate all the more.

'I take it that you are not a fan of McDonald's then?' he said.

The surgeon flexed his shoulder blades and wiped a hand down over his mouth.

'Take a wild guess,' he replied.

Thirty-four

FOUR DAYS AFTER her operation, Emily Buchanan was discharged. The photo of her leaving New York Presbyterian made front-page news from coast to coast. It gave hope to the forty thousand Americans who had so far contracted oculosis, all of them frantic for Dr. Kaine's operation.

Victims of the virus mobbed every eye department in the country. Some of the blind had collapsed on the ground in shock, while others were screaming at anyone who would listen. A great many unaffected citizens had taken to wearing protective goggles that supposedly screened out high-spectrum light. Unscrupulous dealers were selling them online for a fortune, despite the fact that none of them gave any protection at all against oculosis.

Kaine's answering service took many hundreds of calls every hour, the wealthiest sufferers outbidding each other for his services. A handful of potential clients offered a million dollars per eye saved.

Every ophthalmic surgeon in the land had perused Kaine's outline of the operation successfully performed on Emily Buchanan. But none dared replicate it. The risks were so great that even the best surgeons regarded it as foolhardy. Some went so far as to suggest that Kaine and the New York Presbyterian had cooked up the story as some kind of well-timed publicity stunt.

As for the offers, Amadeus Kaine refused them all.

Perched on the sofa in his office, he went through an analysis of the oculosis victims so far. Most of them were aged between twenty and forty-five, equally split between the genders. At least half were employed in some way with food or as homemakers. Most were from lower- or middle-income backgrounds, the kind of families who depended on fast food and on cut-price supermarkets. But despite this, there were plenty of wealthy American homes that had been hit — a hint at the ubiquitous nature of fast food.

All of a sudden Kaine's thoughts turned to the Prime Minister of Tenin. An internet news report that morning had announced that the leader was being sued for not paying his hospital bills. Now that his government had fallen, he was claiming both poverty and asylum.

The doctor considered the feast of fresh eyes he had so enjoyed on the return flight to New York — how they had virtually melted in his mouth. Then, in horror, he reflected on the way society condemned the one food that could nurture the human mind and solve the riddle of oculosis.

Pondering the subject, he began to wonder whether it was just the eye, or if amino acids in other human tissue had a similar effect. Glancing at his wristwatch, an antique Breguet, he was struck by another random thought.

As far as he could see, there had been no cases of oculosis from the intellectual classes. This didn't mean, of course, that there had not been any — but it was strange all the same. The obvious explanation was the link with lower-income homes and cheap processed food.

For more than an hour, Kaine reviewed the latest case studies from the Eastern Seaboard. Then he perused a report from northern California, in which random tests had been carried out on the general population.

Amazingly, ten computer programmers in Silicon Valley had just been discovered as being oculosis positive, but they exhibited no symptoms at all.

It didn't make sense.

Kaine thought back over his career to all the times he had experienced the eye being affected by the brain, and vice versa. He had isolated examples before in which certain people had formed a natural immunity to an illness because of the way they used their brain. Of course it wasn't possible to say for sure that this was the case with oculosis. After all, an individual might have taken up in a line of employment because of a natural propensity, rather than their brain changing as a result of their work.

For a minute or two, Kaine considered flying out to Silicon Valley and running tests there. But, glancing again at the dial of his Breguet, a far more poignant idea struck him.

As a graduate student he had studied under the finest eye surgeon of his generation, a Belgian named Claude-Maurice Rochard. A kind of Hercule Poirot throwback from the Edwardian age, Professor Rochard had made a name for himself by shattering the preconceived ideas of all the surgeons who had come before. Branding them as infidels, they were, he claimed, men who misunderstood the very basis of sight. As he put it, the men who were supposed to be bringing clarity were themselves completely blind.

Rochard's masterwork had considered the way Swiss watchmakers were immune to certain hereditary diseases of both eye and brain. His thesis pivoted on the point that a constant examination of minutiae had a miraculous effect on the neural cortex and on the faculties of the eye.

Kaine stood up, went to the window and stared down at the commuters on Madison Avenue. He loved to watch them, scurrying about like mice. As always, he reflected on how utterly wasted their lives were.

The more he watched them, the more he thought of minutiae, of the watchmakers, and of his teacher.

He went over to the phone and was about to call information for Rochard's number when something made him stop. No, no, the last thing to do was to announce his arrival. The old man had always enjoyed nothing more than surprises, and none more than those of former students.

But how could Kaine be certain he was still alive and living in Paris? It was fifteen years since they had last spoken. Might he have died? Surely Kaine would have heard. Perhaps he had moved away from the apartment on Avenue Franklin Roosevelt?

Kaine swished the air with his hand.

Impossible — Emeritus Professor Rochard would be living it up in the faded grandeur across from the Grand Palais until his last breath.

Kaine booked a ticket on that evening's redeye. Then he took a cab over to the Upper West Side to pay a visit to Bill. If there was no chance of a human eye, at least he hoped to get his hands on a good raw piece of kangaroo meat.

Thirty-five

AT THE CRILLON on the Place de la Concorde, Amadeus Kaine took the Bernstein Suite up on the fifth floor. He was touched that the manager remembered his fondness for its view over Paris towards the Eiffel Tower, especially as he hadn't visited for a decade and a half. The hotel was about to close for a full renovation, leading its many admirers to worry that it would lose the magic and enduring charm.

In the foyer a large poster had been pinned to a board requesting anyone who had recently arrived from North America to identify themselves. At Charles de Gaulle there had been the same second-rate attempt to check up on possible victims of oculosis.

The duty clerk thanked the surgeon for registering himself as an American, and wrote his name in green ink on the pages of a leather-bound ledger.

'We shall inform you, monsieur, if there is word from the authorities,' he said.

'Tell me, have there been any cases of oculosis here in France so far?'

The duty clerk shrugged in a way that only the French can do.

'Here in France, monsieur, we are guilty of many things,' he replied, 'but a love of fast food is not one of them. *Au contraire*, we have constructed an entire culture upon the three-hour lunch.'

Thirty-six

AS FAR AS the eye surgeon was concerned, one of the great joys in life was to know a handful of cities well. Outside the United States there were five places he considered home: Buenos Aires, Tokyo, Cape Town, London, and Paris.

He knew the secret corners and the good restaurants, the little museums where privacy was guaranteed and, best of all, the old friends who lived in ramshackle apartments in each of them. Years or even decades might pass between visits, but it didn't seem to matter at all.

Kaine walked out to Concorde, past the fountains of bronze and gold, then slowly down the Champs Élysées. It was a chill winter afternoon, with a promise of snow in the air. Everyone was wrapped up against the cold, the thrill of Christmas gone and the expectation of spring not quite arrived.

There was not a city in the world that sang to Kaine so sweetly as the French capital. He dreamed of it on nights when he couldn't sleep, or when he was trying to forgive his ex-wife for the shame she had caused him. He smiled at the thought of its belligerent waiters and its pretentiousness, and at the way it ran to a rhythm all of its own.

Unhurried, he walked along the grand boulevard, taking in the life and the detail.

Nearby, a little boy was jumping up and down on a frozen puddle, his father calling him to heel. But the boy wasn't listening. He began doing star jumps, then spinning round and round, his blue rubber boots breaking through to the gravel below.

The plane trees were naked, tortured and forlorn. Even so, there was a stark beauty about them, a kind of natural balance between the profusion of the warm months and the decay of the cold. In the late summer they would be transformed into an undulating canopy of green.

Taking a shortcut to the left, Kaine retraced the steps beneath the trees, steps that were second nature. He had spent two years in Paris while a pupil of Rochard. That was back in the early eighties, when he had a long mane of hair, Converse sneakers, and a penchant for Van Morrison.

The Grand Palais's masonry had been steam cleaned since then. It was tawny yellow now. High above the glass and steel, the mighty tricolour of the Republic was ripping back and forth in the wind.

The shortcut ended in Avenue Franklin Roosevelt, unchanged in decades. It was a little spruced up of course, but in understated magnificence it was just the same.

Rochard resided on the third floor of a building once home to Harriet Howard, the English mistress of Napoleon III.

Crossing the street, Dr. Kaine felt as though he were floating on air. He walked over to the building, number 29, and pushed the door open. *Click.* He stepped through to the short carriageway, the bronze lanterns swaying gently in the draught.

At the second door, a glass one, he searched the names on the buzzers. There were plenty of new ones, some Russian and some Greek. And there it was, bottom right corner, Claude-Maurice Rochard.

Collecting his thoughts, Kaine pressed the buzzer long and hard.

There was a delay, then a stony silence. A dog was barking out in the distance, and a child screaming in its pushchair out on the street.

Then an old man's voice blared through the intercom.
'Oui?'
'Professor Rochard?'
'Oui?' The voice was more quizzical.
'This is Amadeus Kaine.'
The voice grunted, coughed, and said:

'I was wondering just this morning when you'd turn up. It's the third floor as you know.'

There was a loud buzz and the glass door swung open.

Thirty-seven

THE DRAB, UNPAINTED walls of Professor Rochard's apartment were hung with a series of enormous oil studies of the human eye. Some were no more than blurs, while others were acutely observed, their colours quite shocking and bright. They had been executed a century before by a depressive Parisian called Hugo Mostaut. He had fallen under the wheels of a train while drunk, and had bled to death because no surgeon could be found brave enough to treat his wounds in time.

The paintings were auctioned at the Hotel George V on the very last day of the war. There had been no bids for them, except that of the young Rochard. He had bought the entire lot for a hundred francs, and they had inspired him to make a career in ophthalmology.

The doctor may have aged, but he had done so with style. His hair was shiny white, and his complexion had a ruddy vigour, as if he had defied the Reaper.

'I'm ninety-one,' he said pouring whiskies for them both. 'And I feel like fifty-three.'

Kaine laughed hard.

'And I'm fifty-three,' he replied, 'but feel that I'm ninety-one.'

'You don't look so bad, and you'd look a great deal better if you shook the burdens of the world from your shoulders. Anyway, it serves you right for forgetting me.'

The professor let out a cackle.

'I didn't forget,' said Kaine quickly. 'I just thought I'd leave you in peace.'

'I heard you got divorced.'

'Yes. And thank God for it. She didn't approve of...' he stopped mid-sentence and sipped his whisky — a rare single malt. He sighed.

'So you've heard about it, about oculosis?' he said.

'I may be old,' said Rochard, 'but I'm neither deaf nor blind. I'm keeping abreast of the situation, and am just surprised it didn't come sooner.'

'*Chickens...* the vector is chickens, I'm sure of it.'

'Yes, of course it is. But what surprise is that?'

'None at all.'

'The world out there — *your* world over there... it doesn't appear to consider it a surprise.'

'They look at the detail and not the big picture,' said Kaine. 'You taught me that. It's what makes them blind.'

'Our race has been blind for centuries, but only now the blindness has changed its form. Now we're all surprised by it.'

Amadeus Kaine sat down on a wide fauteuil and allowed his eyes to trace the zigzags of the parquet. He got a flash of his childhood, of his father sitting on the porch of their summer home out at Cape Cod. Then he blinked and the memory was gone.

'I've noticed something,' he said.

'What?'

'That the virus doesn't seem to be affecting those with a propensity for technical detail. It reminded me of your thesis — the watchmakers.'

Rochard poured himself another malt, a double. He slugged it back in one.

'Tell me that it surprises you.'

'I guess it doesn't. It's what you've been saying all along — that intellectual stimulation has a resounding effect on the eye.'

'It affects it in ways science has never imagined,' Rochard said sternly.

'But how's it going to help all the millions of poor bastards who are now going blind from oculosis?'

'It's not. Stimulation now would be too little, too late.'

'Naturally.'

'So what to do?'

'I operated the other day on one of the first victims, a young woman. Managed to restore her sight by passing a minimal electric current into the iris.'

'The Slaverly Process?'

'Yes.'

'And it worked?'

'It did indeed. But it's the tip of the iceberg.'

Professor Rochard crept over to the fire and stoked the coals. He peered into the great gilded mirror above the marble mantelpiece, saw his former pupil reflected in it behind him.

'I sense that I am rather like you,' he said slowly, 'in that I have little sympathy for the masses the world over who stuff their gullets with the processed filth they call food.'

Kaine smiled, a smile that worked itself into a grin.

'It was you who first introduced me to the concept of obscure cuisine,' he said.

Rochard winked.

'Good, isn't it?'

'It opened up a new world, a realm of flavour and texture that I never believed possible. Take my word for it, I have discovered foods that perform nothing less than magic on the mind.'

Professor Rochard sat down on the couch and ran a hand down the back of an old ginger tom that had appeared from the shadows near the door.

'Oculosis may be a blessing in disguise,' he said.

'You really think so?'

'Why not? It's merely nature making a correction.'

'I suppose so.'

The professor coughed, took a deep breath, and smiled.

'Humans have become so weakened,' he said. 'It's pathetic. I'm ashamed of our race, horrified by all the spineless wimps out there. We're no longer on the savannah, fighting for our lives. We're weak and wretched…'

'But at the same time we hold the future of the planet in our hands. And the planet's biting back.'

'Of course it is! It's wounded and in the throes of death! If I were the Earth, I'd smite the whole lot of us and begin again!'

'Another Noah's Ark?'

'No, no — I'm talking about *total* annihilation. It's the only way.'

'It looks as though that may actually happen,' Kaine said, staring into the flames. 'I can work it out though,' he added in a whisper. 'I am certain I can find a cure.'

'Then what's stopping you?'

'The right food.'

'What?'

'The right food for my brain.'

Thirty-eight

AMADEUS KAINE HAD spent only an hour with Rochard before the old professor emeritus grew tired and had to rest. At the end of the visit he wondered whether it had been worth making the journey at all.

Of course it had — not just to be in the great man's presence once again, but because it had spelled out in Kaine's own mind what he had to do.

Like Rochard, he was repulsed by the way his fellow Americans gorged themselves on mountains of the lowest-grade food. They covered it all in the cheapest processed cheese, gave it fancy names, and then wondered why they ballooned out so greatly that they couldn't walk. It was muck, all of it — muck unfit for pigs. And oculosis was simply nature's correction — a warning shot fired across the bows of American society.

But Kaine had an answer.

It may have been taboo in every society on Earth, yet it was the one definite answer — an answer to get an answer.

Snow was falling lightly by the time he left the apartment on Avenue Franklin Roosevelt. It was dark, or rather, it was grey. The clouds hung low over the Champs Élysées, the sound of cars on the cobbles muffled and somehow remote.

Having made his way back to the Place de la Concorde, Kaine was about to cross the street to the Crillon when something stopped him. Turning on his heel, he made his way down to the Seine.

As he walked along the riverbank on autopilot, his mind was soothed by the patterns of light streaming over the water's rippled surface and by the eddies of snow. He got a flash of Madison Avenue and then of Drusnev clutching a platter of pastries filled with eyes. Then he thought about Emily Buchanan and that he had saved her from eternal darkness.

It was nothing new, that sense of power. Every surgeon who has ever saved a life or restored injured ability has experienced it. But it had been made possible by a great leap in consciousness — a leap itself achieved by the last taboo.

The next hour was one Kaine processed time and again in the weeks that followed. It was as though he were acting out a pre-ordained plan, as if he were not in control.

Taking care not to slip, he walked along the towpath until he came to the nightclub beneath Pont Alexandre III. The club was closed, locked up tight for the winter freeze.

The snow was falling more heavily now in large, dry crystals. Kaine caught two or three on his hand and felt them melt away. Then he sought refuge beneath the bridge. There was no one there, not a soul. In a strange way it seemed like the loneliest place in the world.

All of a sudden, the surgeon began shaking.

He had no idea why, because he wasn't really cold. Rather, he was warm, or baking hot — as he had been after swallowing the excised eye in the hospital.

He stood there, his back pressed up against the stone wall, quite certain of exactly what to do. The blueprint of his next actions was laid out neatly in his mind. The wind swept up and howled down the river. There was rage in it, fury, and bitter tangles of falling snow — a tempestuous expression of nature.

The outside world was suddenly masked out in sheets of white.

Then, an emaciated young woman emerged from the blizzard. She was dressed in little more than rags, her bare feet in broken sandals. Her arms were bare as well, bruised and punctured, emerald eyes hanging in a hollow face. Crouching in the corner beneath the great iron balustrades, she eased a blunt needle into her ankle.

Kaine watched, fascinated. They hadn't acknowledged each other — two random strangers taking refuge in the same spot.

The wind was screeching now, as if a harbinger of some primeval time. The snow spun and eddied under the sides of the bridge, melting as it came to rest on stone. Amadeus Kaine was overcome. He felt strong and vital, as though an ancient power had been breathed into him.

Without giving it consideration or thought, he strode over to the addict and snapped her neck.

She slumped instantly to the ground, her body hitting the flagstones without the least grunt of a noise. Then, bending over, the doctor sucked out her eyes.

The left, then the right.

In freeze-frame he savoured the moment, the taste, the texture, the rush of human flesh. It felt so perfect, so natural, as though every other man alive had somehow become separated from the true path.

Wiping his mouth with the back of his hand, Kaine held the girl's face before him. The eye sockets were hollow but somehow quite serene. He had released her from a life of torment, of misery, and was proud to have been of service. As he looked at her, taking in the smallest details of her face, the frenzy of elation kicked in.

What to do with her?

The eye surgeon thought fast, his mind fortified by the feast. Dozens of cadavers are found in the Seine every year — a fact universally known. She would be just another, her eyes pecked out by starving winter crows. Lifting her from the stone floor with one hand, he raised her in an arc past his nose, breathing her in.

She smelled of aged garlic.

Conjuring all his strength, he thrust her into the cold water. The corpse hardly made a sound as it plopped beneath the surface. Given the current, Kaine imagined it would be swept well downstream by the time it was discovered.

He looked up, checking whether there was a CCTV camera outside the club. There was one, but vandals had taken care of it long ago.

His mind hurtling with vivid colours, sounds, and thoughts, Amadeus Kaine made his way calmly back to the Bernstein Suite in the warmth of the Hotel Crillon.

Thirty-nine

WITHIN A DAY of the addict's death, Dr. Kaine was back in his apartment on the Upper East Side. He might have cherished Paris as one does the memory of a first love, but it wasn't his home. He appreciated the way that New Yorkers were encouraged to be individuals, while delighting in being a kind of fraternity of their own making.

As he saw it, they were pitted against all other Americans — somehow superior, able to deal with the kind of stress and suffering non-existent elsewhere. Kaine believed the result was a city that was a kind of open-air science lab, an experiment that defied reason.

And it was the strains of lunacy that kept him there.

All those loners ambling about Central Park talking to themselves, or the guys stalking the shelves of drugstores in the early hours, or the weirdos who lived on cans of chilled cat food — they were part of a secret race, a race that gave New York solid cultural depth. Paris had the beauty, the serenity and the *bonne vie*, but it didn't have the psycho zone — a point that Amadeus Kaine regarded as a crying shame.

The day after his return, he rolled up his sleeves and got down to work in training other surgeons to operate on oculosis. He was surprised by their lack of understanding, and that they hadn't sought out answers for themselves. With the odds stacked so horribly against them, they had folded, collapsed, waited for someone else to come up with a workable solution.

And in Kaine they had found that someone.

Each morning for a week, the eye surgeon operated on oculosis cases. They were chosen at random from the legions of victims who couldn't afford to pay.

The offers may still have been coming in thick and fast from rich Americans who had contracted the disease, but Kaine wasn't interested in them at all. He was disgusted by them. Just because they had money — a great deal of money — they imagined they had a right to his services.

In the afternoons, after surgery, Kaine met with others from his profession, and he taught them. They convened in person at special sessions and by video link. Films of the treatments were made available to teaching hospitals across the nation. Within a week, other surgeons were attempting the Slaverly Process.

About half the cases undertaken failed, a result of the misunderstanding surrounding the complexities of the procedure.

Each night, Kaine returned to his apartment and watched the spread of oculosis on the news. Every chicken in the country had been slaughtered, and ordinary members of the public were demanding the culling of other livestock as well.

Hysteria had descended over the country, hysteria aimed squarely at poultry and eggs.

Recipes containing either of them were shunned. As chefs resorted to finding new foods to replace them, every last chicken and egg was rooted out and destroyed.

The most worrying thing of all was how society was disintegrating. Robbed of their sight, tens of thousands of people had become victims of layers of unscrupulous subculture. Thievery, mugging and murder had risen exponentially, as anyone with a grievance took advantage of the collapsing systems to take revenge.

The National Guard was called out, and the president went on TV, declaring that he would fight oculosis as though he was fighting the scourge of terror. Rallying Americans, he cajoled them to pull together as one.

But night after night, Amadeus Kaine watched as the fabric of honest, God-fearing society was torn apart. TV evangelists likened oculosis to a biblical plague, and used the virus to gain support across the Deep South. A sense of animosity prevailed, and raw suspicion, too, with armed vigilante groups patrolling every neighbourhood.

The eye surgeon found himself charged with a sense of duty, one he had never really appreciated before. Realizing that he could himself effect a change, he worked harder than he had ever done in his life.

But all the while he thought of the addict's emerald eyes.

He thought of them when he was in the cab on the way to Mount Sinai each morning, and when he was scrubbing up. He thought of them, too, when he was operating on the endless oculosis patients, and when he was lecturing in the long, damp afternoons. He even thought of them in the shower, and when he was lying in bed waiting for sleep to take him each night.

They had been so different from the other eyes. The colour had been remarkable, yes, but the difference had run far deeper. It was linked to the texture, taste and, most importantly, to the rush.

For the first time in his fifty-three years, the girl's eyes had provided Amadeus Kaine with real vision.

He remembered having read a book about *ayahuasca*, the flora-based hallucinogen of the Upper Amazon. Taken by the Shuar, a tribe of former headshrinkers, the remedy gave them a sense that they were growing wings and flying — flying into what they considered to be the 'real' world. It was exactly the same thing with the green eyes — the sense of ascending into reality, leaving the humdrum world of illusion behind.

But there was a problem.

While the green eyes' rush had been quite astonishing, it hadn't lasted more than a day and a half. And, when it had gone, the doctor was left with a shattering sense of withdrawal. He had never understood the suicidal, but he was suddenly ready to join their ranks. Struggling to get a grip, he gulped down painkillers, anti-depressants, and all manner of other prescription drugs. Nothing could alleviate the terrible sense of self-loathing and loss.

It was at this point that the celebrated surgeon's counting obsessions reached a new and disturbing height. As the hours wore on, he counted both visible and invisible objects, as well as ideas and metaphors, names, and postulations of the most fanciful nature. He became fixated with chewing the skin on his fingertips, too, and with staring out at the winter sun.

As a medical man, Kaine knew these were signs of madness. But however bizarre the extended rituals and compulsions were, they gave rigidity and a framework to his life. And the one thing he needed now was structure, however flimsy.

Lose it and the world around him was likely to collapse.

Forty

ONE NIGHT, AFTER a long day at Mount Sinai, the surgeon went home, put on his French linen pyjamas, and poured himself a glass of Hautes-Côtes de Beaune. Having taken a gulp and swilled the precious liquid around his mouth, he turned on the television.

After flicking channels for a moment, he reached BBC America. There was a special bulletin from the English countryside where oculosis had taken hold, and where poultry was now being slaughtered en masse.

A reporter was standing outside the Half Moon Public House in the market town of Shaftesbury. Amadeus Kaine recognized it at once. He had stayed nearby on honeymoon, in a thatched cottage off the high street. It was the one happy memory he had of being with Francine.

The reporter said that oculosis was spreading across Europe like a plague and was now threatening hundreds of thousands of people. She likened it to the Black Death in the way it was reducing a functioning system to outright anarchy.

Switching the television off, Kaine changed back into his regular clothes and put on his overcoat. He was frustrated, his hands moving fast with the buttons and then with the leather laces of his brogues. The frustration arose from the sense of grave responsibility. As he saw it, he was in a land of imbeciles, and was the one man alive with a functioning brain. Certain that oculosis could be treated without surgery, he was adamant that it was merely a matter of making the right connections.

Leave it to the masses though, and there wasn't a hope in hell.

Amadeus Kaine went downstairs. Greeting the doorman, he asked him about the vacation he was planning to take with his elderly wife, before sweeping out into the street. A minute later he was walking north on Park Avenue, his mind on one thing alone.

Green eyes.

The addict beneath Pont Alexandre III had for a short while changed his psychology in the most fundamental way. For a few fleeting hours he had been Einstein, or Aristotle, Da Vinci, Newton, Beethoven or Shakespeare — or the whole lot of them rolled into one.

But by the time he came to terms with the genius at his fingertips, the power was beginning to fade.

He knew it was wrong, but Kaine needed the power back.

Without it there was no hope of ever thrashing the scourge of oculosis. The human race would be resigned to living in darkness for eternity. It was a future that was no more than a few wretched steps away.

But where to find green eyes?

The eye surgeon had considered going online, making a date with a call girl, filtering the results by eye colour. It was an ingenious idea, but one which would have taken too long to set up.

He needed green eyes right away.

As for a preference in gender or age, he didn't really have one. He wasn't going to eat the eyes for some bizarre sexual turn-on, or for psychopathic thrills. His need was far more elemental. It was about the effect of certain amino acids on the mind.

All he could think about was the colour. The deeper the shade of green, the better.

In the left pocket of his overcoat was a small wooden box. His fingers caressed it as he walked. Hidden inside was a pair of curved slivers of glass. They had been the first he ever made, and were the only objects connected to eye surgery that Kaine kept in his apartment.

The streets were almost deserted.

Terrified by the thought of contracting oculosis, most New Yorkers had bolted themselves up at home. Dozens of stores had closed up or employed armed officers to guard the doors. A few had even gone so far as to supply their employees with ski masks and protective suits.

Turning right onto East 86th Street, Kaine was surprised to find the Fairway open for business as usual. The alternative supermarket was the one general source of food he trusted, although it carried next to nothing in obscure cuisine.

Outside, a couple of employees were packing up the fruit and veg. Both of them were sporting cheap plastic overalls and what appeared to be swimming goggles. They seemed drained and confused, and were huffing and puffing in the cold. Making his way past them slowly, the surgeon struggled to get a glimpse of the colour of their eyes.

Both had dark brown.

Striding on into the store, Kaine walked casually to the back. It was brighter there. He pretended to be searching for Marmite, a British brand of yeast extract. Three more sales staff helped him, all women with yet more brown eyes, all of them hidden behind identical swimming goggles.

Suddenly, he noticed a young man with a limp, pulling a shopping cart behind him.

Kaine looked around slowly.

Blue-grey eyes. He cursed. Damn New Yorkers, he thought, when you wanted them to deliver on something they always came up short.

For twenty minutes he stalked the aisles and counters. At last he spotted a woman who was mumbling to herself. She had mousy brown hair and was well below average height, with a pale face, reddish cheeks, and delightful olive-green eyes. She must have been thirty, but she looked younger.

Kaine glanced into her basket and frowned.

She had no idea of what to eat, he thought, despite the fact she was shopping at the Fairway. Still mumbling, she glanced at him as she passed.

'I see you like Marmite,' he said.

The woman blushed.

'I lived in England. I know it's an acquired taste, but I guess I acquired it, along with a love for English weather and hot buttered scones.'

'I adore it — Marmite, I mean,' said the doctor.

He took half a step forward so that the woman could see a large jar of it in his own basket. She was attracted to him — he could feel it by the way she leaned in and looked down.

'You have the most beautiful eyes,' he said.

'Thank you.'

'It must sound like a pickup line, but I assure you I'm not at the Fairway just before midnight on the prowl.' He let out half a laugh.

'You look as though you just got home from work.'

'That's right. I did.'

'What do you do?' she asked as if hardly caring.

'I'm a surgeon, an eye surgeon.'

The woman appeared almost frightened.

'It's awful, what's happening with the illness… with oc…'

'*Oculosis.*'

'Yes,' she paused, blushed again, and held out a small pale hand.

'I'm Marcie,' she said.

'Good to meet you, Marcie. My name is Amadeus Kaine.'

Forty-one

WITHIN AN HOUR of leaving the Fairway, Marcie was dead, her neck snapped like that of the addict beneath Pont Alexandre III. She hadn't suspected a thing, not even when the surgeon had nudged up close as they walked. Choosing his moment, he waited until they were under scaffolding between Lexington and Park Avenue. Then, quickly, he slipped behind her and separated the second and third cervical vertebrae.

Jerking his victim into a doorway beneath the scaffolding, he pulled on the yellow rubber washing-up gloves he had bought at the store, then sucked out Marcie's eyes and swallowed them whole. Then, removing the glass eyes from the box, he forced them nimbly into place. No one alive could quell ocular blood-flow or insert glass eyes as expertly as he.

Almost at once Amadeus Kaine could think with total clarity.

It was as though he had been a zombie just moments before. Churning away at lightning speed, his mind processed everything his eyes showed him.

He looked down at the smooth concrete beneath his feet and wondered why the city didn't ripple it gently so that people wouldn't slip in the winter months. And the scaffolding poles — why weren't they covered with a phosphorescent paint so that they were more conspicuous in the dark? But there was no time to solve all New York's problems right then.

Kaine had problems of his own to deal with.

Quickly, he stuffed Marcie's purse into his coat pocket, and threw her body into the workmen's dumpster, covering it with rubble. Then, taking a cab down to Mount Sinai, he entered the hospital through a back door.

Once there, he made sure to ask the clerk on duty whether his ID had been found, so that he would be remembered in case an alibi were required.

By 2.25 a.m. he was back home, his mind racing as it had never raced before. Unable to sleep, he paced up and down counting numbers on his fingers and reciting the alphabet backwards. He was gripped by a sense of euphoria, as though the world were a paradise, a realm untouched by the shortcomings of man.

As for taking the life of another innocent victim, he didn't feel bad about it in the least. In truth, Kaine hardly gave it a passing thought. Marcie had made a small sacrifice, allowing him a burst of unmitigated genius — genius that could now be harnessed for the good of all mankind.

The eye surgeon spent the remainder of the night with his fingertips pressed together, sitting forward in a cabriole chair. He went back through every memory and printed word he had ever read — piecing together a treasure trail of clues that would help solve the riddle of viral oculosis.

The next morning, after no sleep, Kaine discarded Marcie's purse in a garbage bin near the East River, and then he made his way back down to Mount Sinai for another session of surgery.

Peering into the eyes of the morning's first patient, he suddenly had a flash of inspiration, and found himself regarding oculosis in an entirely new light. As the surgical team stood around awaiting orders, Amadeus Kaine burst out laughing.

'Is everything OK, doctor?' asked a nurse hesitantly.

'I don't believe it.'

'What?'

'That I've been so stupid, so damned blind.'

The nurse looked over at the anaesthetist and shrugged.

Kaine completed the operation in ten minutes, restoring the patient's sight in both eyes.

'We're done here,' he said, pulling away his mask.

'Already?'

'Yes, nurse, *already*.'

'But...'

'But I thought of a more efficient method.'

'Just like that?'

'Yes nurse, just like that.'

Forty-two

By LUNCHTIME, KAINE's breakthrough was headline news on all the networks. The eye surgeon was mobbed as he left Mount Sinai that afternoon, a swarm of reporters rushing up with microphones. Standing just outside the hospital, he was immediately engulfed.

'Is it true that you've beaten oculosis, doctor?' shouted a reporter in a Mexican accent.

'Is oculosis a thing of the past?' yelled another.

Kaine pinched a thumb and forefinger to the cufflink on his right wrist and took a sharp breath.

'Don't jump to conclusions,' he said. 'All I've done is to develop a kind of short-cut treatment.'

'What does it mean for all the sufferers across America?'

'It means that other surgeons can use the technique and make a real difference.'

A journalist pushed his way to the front. He was wearing an old raincoat and a trilby, and had a digital recorder in his hand.

'Can you tell readers of the *New York Times* why oculosis struck?'

Kaine held out a hand.

'I believe that this disease is just the first in a multitude of afflictions that will be visited on the American population in the coming decades,' he said.

'But why us? Is it related to the War on Terror? Is it a new threat dreamt up by al-Qaeda?'

'Look at us,' shouted Amadeus Kaine. 'We live in a mechanized, industrialized society. We use machines to do everything, and we think that we can create food by the same mass industrialization. It's lunacy. We've become detached from the Earth of our ancestors, and oculosis is nature reminding us of that.'

Forty-three

EARLY THAT EVENING, Kaine went to his office and leafed through the pile of unopened mail. He couldn't imagine going back to the old routine of neurotic VIP patients and despotic dictators with their feeble anxieties and invented woes. They were sapping his strength and wasting a brilliant career.

He turned on the lights in the lab and checked his stock of glass rods. Mrs. Phelps might have driven him half mad, but she was good at keeping stock levels in order. There must have been enough glass to make fifty glass eyes, with pigments for any imaginable shade of iris.

Removing his jacket, the surgeon swapped it for his old lab coat. Then he set about conjuring the most perfect pair of glass eyes. Choosing the colour with care, a delicate Limoges blue, he set to work warming the gather under the flame.

Any colour would have been fine, so long as it wasn't green.

At 9.20 p.m. the surgeon slept for three hours, waking in a calm, rested frame of mind. The effect of Marcie's eyes was already on the wane. It was as though he was building up a kind of tolerance. He thought back to the first human eye, the one in the very first pie, and how long its effect had lasted.

As Kaine pondered it, there was a distinct possibility that green eyes had a far shorter impact than other colours, but they released such a charge of enlightenment that they were worth the extra trouble.

Soon after midnight, he placed the newly made glass eyes, a pair of surgical gloves, and a Kaine Excisor in a dark blue daypack. Then he turned off the lights and made his way down to the street.

For the next three hours he roamed Manhattan, dodging the vigilante gangs that were now prowling the streets.

Buoyed by adrenalin, he felt strangely light-headed. At the same time he saw the world around him with an astonishing sense of clarity.

There were flashbacks, too.

He could remember climbing trees down in Brooklyn with Bill McMarsh and chugging down a bottle of stolen whiskey with him in Central Park. How old were they then? He squinted into the memory — fourteen, fifteen?

He walked northwards on Park Avenue until he reached 125th Street. There were vigilantes everywhere, battling the legions of petty thieves and muggers. The pungent stink of oily smoke from burning cars hung low over the streets, and the ubiquitous squeal of car alarms was punctuated from time to time by hysterical screams.

Amadeus Kaine turned left and hurried down Martin Luther King Jr. Boulevard. In his mind he was counting the squares of a chessboard, multiplying each one by six and a half. As he did so, he found himself sucked deep into another world, a world that had become his reality.

In the dozens of blocks that passed beneath his feet, he registered almost nothing at all. He was normally so utterly fastidious, such a connoisseur of the insignificant. But on the night of the long walk north it was memory that constructed the architecture of his thoughts.

He thought about his mother and his father.

They had been good people — well mannered and quite unnecessarily kind. But Kaine had never really understood them. Given good educations and sufficient resources, neither had bothered to push themselves, to excel. They had been mediocre people. And the one thing the eye surgeon despised was mediocrity. Most of all, it angered the son that the parents had not had obituaries when they died.

In his mind, every man and woman over thirty should aspire to have a long obituary — preferably in the *New York Times*. Not to be featured in its hallowed pages was, in his mind, to be a loser — a wretched and humiliated subject of contempt.

It was like having never lived at all.

As he walked, Kaine remembered reading of an Afghan family in which, at birth, a child's name was added in pencil to the family tree. Only if that infant achieved real success in adulthood was the name over-written in ink. If he was a disappointment, the name was quietly erased from the lineage and his existence was forgotten.

Amadeus Kaine crossed Second Avenue and cursed the mediocrity of it all. There was nothing of any merit for dozens of blocks, only wastrels and profligates. Consuming their eyes was certainly no loss.

As he walked, he considered how he was doing humanity a grand service. Through his own inimitable brand of genius he had discovered a kind of portal to a new existence. It was one that he imagined must have been known to the ancients but had been lost knowledge for centuries. Through a stroke of luck, revealed in part by the deranged antics of the Supreme Leader Vladimir Drusnev, he had happened upon the one hope left. Without it, mankind was surely destined for a miserable future, one of darkness and futility.

Thanking the universe for sending him to the supreme leader, Kaine began counting again. This time it was multiples of nine. Very soon he had passed five thousand. Then, all of a sudden, he spotted a large convenience store across the street. A towering sentry stood to the left of the door. Stretched between his hands was the shaft of an axe, and over his face was a wool balaclava.

Doing his best to nod a greeting, Kaine pushed past into the store, the daypack slung casually over his shoulder.

Inside it was bright, with security cameras in every corner. The back area was devoted to a large display of hard liquor, arranged in a kind of cage, along with the cigarettes and the sales clerk. He had an angry face that seemed to express how sick he was of working nights in what wasn't far from being a war zone.

He watched the eye surgeon keenly as he moved up and down the aisles.

'You gonna buy somethin'?!' he yelled.

'I'm looking,' said Kaine.

'What for?'

'For a particular product.'

'What?!'

'It's got a greenish cover.'

The clerk screwed up his face and jerked a thumb towards the door.

'Get out of here!'

Kaine felt his back warm with fury, but he coaxed himself to stay calm. He made his way past the freezer packed with ready meals and was soon at the door. Pushing it open a little wider than he needed to, he made way for a wino on his way in. Reeling from side to side, the wino found that the rectangular doorway posed him a severe spatial challenge.

In the fraction of a second as the drunk moved from darkness into the bright neon interior, Kaine looked into his eyes.

He couldn't believe it.

Another stroke of luck.

Pupils dilated from drink, the irises were a deep moss green.

The doctor went out and waited across the street. No one entered or exited the store for fifteen minutes. Squinting from the shadows, he could see the drunk chit-chatting to the clerk, as though they were friends.

Another five minutes slipped by, and the wino lurched out through the door, past the guard. Under his arm was an oversized brown paper bag. Swaying down the street, he paused to steady himself against a wall. Then he threw up before continuing a little faster in the direction of the Harlem River Park.

Amadeus Kaine followed at a discreet distance.

He had not been to the park before. It was an agreeable enough place and, despite the darkness, the half-moon gave satisfactory light. Gradually, it broke through an oval aperture in the clouds.

Dr. Kaine couldn't get over his good fortune. After all, only two per cent of the American population had green eyes. But, as he pondered it, perhaps it wasn't just down to luck.

He had begun to believe that it was through a heightened sensitivity, as much as by luck alone, that he had encountered the drunk. Turning the idea around in his mind, he realized that he had known the man had green eyes even before he had set eyes on his face. He had sensed their existence instinctively, in the same way that menstruating women have been known to sense the presence of snakes.

The drunk flopped down on the first bench he came to, screwed off the top of the vodka bottle, and put the rim to his parched lips. He took a good long gulp, then another, and a third. He burped, coughed, and spat into the dark.

The surgeon moved in slowly, covering the space between himself and the bench with measured circumspection. He didn't want to rush things. Experience had taught him that drunks react unfavourably to quick movement. They can't process speed.

Sliding forward in a kind of slow-mo, Kaine reeled about as if also drunk. It was a plan designed to put the wino at ease.

'Good evenin' to ya!' said the man, a veil of the Emerald Isle shadowing his words.

'Hello, how are you?' said the doctor.

'Not bad, meself. Missing home and just out for a little wander.'

'You're from…'

'From Galway — from out west.'

'A fine part of the world,' said Kaine. 'Land of Poitin.'

'You know the Emerald Nectar?'

'Oh, yes, had it when I was travelling through Connemara.'

'You've been to Connemara?'

The surgeon looked at the drunk, his eyes locking onto his.

'Oh yes,' he said in a calm, even voice. 'I know it quite well.'

The wino held the bottle in Kaine's direction.

'Go on, have a sip,' he said.

'I would, but I think I saw a cop over there.'

The drunk Irishman jerked upright, as though someone had plugged him into an electrical socket.

'Where? Where is 'e then?'

'I saw him heading this way,' Kaine said. 'I know, why don't we go over there into the trees? We can have a nice little drink there. What do you think?'

'Yes!' exclaimed the drunk mischievously. 'A splendid idea!'

The eye surgeon thrust a hand under the man's arm and guided him off the bench and into the darkness. Within a minute or two they were standing between a young elm tree and a bush. Again, the wino offered the bottle's rim. And this time, Kaine took a swig. He choked.

'That's good stuff,' he said.

'I'd say so meself,' whispered the drunk.

And they were the last words he ever said.

In the privacy of the park, Kaine used his Excisor to suck out the Irishman's eyes, having broken his neck. He was salivating heavily but he forced himself to wait. Inspired by his victim's delight in alcohol, he had the idea of enjoying the eyes with a little aperitif.

Stowing them in his little wooden box, and positioning the glass prosthetics in the Irishman's face, Kaine pushed the body as forcefully as he could into the bush. It made very little sound as it went.

Then, congratulating himself, the eye surgeon retreated to the comfort of his apartment. He walked ten blocks south, down to 119th Street with Lexington. And from there he took a cab to the Upper East Side. It amazed him that in a city collapsing from the effect of oculosis, yellow cabs were still running.

By the time the driver pulled over just north of 775 Park Avenue, Kaine was hyperventilating, shaking, babbling, like an opium addict chasing the dragon. The last thing he wanted was to make a clumsy entrance into the prestigious address, and so he stood outside for more than a minute composing himself.

Relaxing his back muscles, he whipped out his mobile phone. It may have been the middle of the night, but everyone knew him to be an important surgeon — one who had just had a breakthrough in the war against oculosis.

Pressing the phone to his cheek, he hurried through the lobby, giving advice to an imaginary surgeon on the other end.

The doorman looked up from his newspaper and nodded.

Two minutes later, Kaine was inside his apartment up on the sixth floor. Removing his overcoat and brogues, he put on a Prelude by Bach and washed his hands three times, with different soaps.

Then, and only then, did he take out a bottle of Armagnac. It was a fine one, from the house of Nismes-Delclou — the 1905 vintage. He had kept it for years, imagining it with a prune and hare pie. But why save it any longer, now that the perfect hors d'oeuvre was about to be served?

Pouring a little of the amber liqueur, he moved it around the sides of the glass, breathing it in. But didn't taste it. Not yet. He wanted the little snack to be perfect in every way.

In the kitchen he transferred the green eyes onto a silver saucer. He had bought it in a Prague flea market a decade before. They looked serene there, as though the metal receptacle had been awaiting them all its life.

Kaine wondered whether the eyes ought to be warmed. He considered poaching them, or heating them gently in the oven. No, no — heat would damage the delicate capillaries. And besides, he couldn't wait.

He speed-counted to nine hundred in multiples of three.

Taking the silver dish through into the sitting room, he slid it onto the coffee table. Then he placed the glass in front of it and a little to the right.

He counted to sixty.

Unable to wait a moment longer, he licked his lips and ate the eyes one at a time, before taking a long, satisfying sip of Armagnac.

Leaning back in his chair, the surgeon allowed the sense of ecstasy to cascade over him. It was like being baptized in the waters of immortality, or being pulled into the bosom of nature.

How could he ever be satisfied by the food of mortals again?

Forty-four

THE FOLLOWING MORNING, a Saturday, Kaine lay in bed until nine-thirty. An habitual early riser, he was the kind of man who beat himself up with guilt for wasting time at being horizontal. Switching on the radio news, he caught the end of a report about oculosis. There was nothing else being covered, not even on the escalating troubles with Pyongyang — the one corner of the world so far unaffected by the virus.

A fresh outbreak had occurred in a small Nebraskan town. What was strange about it was the way the infection had spread. Whereas the initial oculosis victims tended to lose sight in the right eye, and then the left, the Nebraskan cases went blind in both eyes at once. And more than half of those affected were children under ten.

Oculosis was mutating, and this was the first proof.

Amadeus Kaine got out of bed, put on his robe and sat in a pool of sunshine, a laptop balanced on his knees. A quick search brought up fifteen more cases of the mutation — in Taipei, Canberra, Durban, and Stockholm. In at least one of them the iris had dissolved within a day and a half — making any treatment quite impossible.

His stomach rumbling, Kaine shuffled through to the kitchen. He got down to cooking up his routine weekend breakfast of eggs on toast. But his stomach turned at the thought.

It was rumbling because it wanted eyes, not eggs.

Forty-five

LATER THAT MORNING, still having not eaten, the doctor checked his email. There were two hundred and sixty requests for interviews and surgical help from around the world. The media and the medical community considered Amadeus Kaine the one man alive who could come up with a cure for oculosis. With no one else to turn to, they had begun to regard him almost as a messianic figure. The strange thing was that Kaine regarded himself as exactly that as well.

When it came to the human eye, he had no doubt he was a miracle worker of the highest order. But to perform miracles he needed green eyes, and plenty of them.

It was a simple matter of *quid pro quo*.

Rising from the chair, he placed the laptop down on the table and walked over to the window in thought. America was in a state of crisis — far worse than anything it had ever faced. If the endless predictions were right, the oculosis virus would hit eighty per cent of the population within five months. Kaine may have refined his treatment, but it was sure to lose efficacy as the disease mutated, as it had already done in Nebraska.

It may have seemed extreme, but he considered contacting the FBI and instructing them of his culinary need. The way he saw it, the world was back to front. Everyone out there with any medical training ought to have been eating human eyes. It was the only way to reverse impending catastrophe.

Forty-six

ALL THAT AFTERNOON, he worked away in his laboratory making glass eyes. Blowing each one perfectly by hand took time, but it calmed him, and gave him time to think.

A skilled craft dating back to Ancient Egyptian times, the process of making prosthetic eyes was, Kaine believed, terribly underappreciated. Most surgeons couldn't be bothered with them any more, resorting to cheap plastic lenses churned out by machines in India and the Far East. As Kaine saw it, glass was not only more natural, but it somehow brought the surgeon and the patient together in a kind of unbreakable contract.

By the end of the afternoon twelve pairs of eyes were cooling on the stand. Some were light blue, others dark brown, hazel, or grey. None of them were green. After all, the last thing he wanted was to make it easier for the authorities to trace his victims.

Until then, Kaine had made sure that he had relieved them of their ID, but he knew it was only a matter of time before one of them was discovered to be fitted with prosthetic eyes.

Over the next week, Kaine took a life each night.

He began travelling out by train to the suburbs, where he found it far easier to get victims alone — victims with fine green eyes. The more he killed, the easier he found it, until he was so expert at snapping necks that he could do it while thinking of something else. He wondered why the world of crime didn't learn a little basic biology. Were it to do so, criminals everywhere would be snapping necks and would do away with their guns.

On most nights he brought the eyes home and ate them with a glass of wine or an Armagnac. He found that Malbec and Rioja went very well with them, as did a sprinkling of Caspian caviar. Best of all, however, was to cover them in truffle oil, and to eat them with a warmed soup spoon, washing them down with a glass or two of '83 Petrus.

The more eyes he consumed, the more he began to appreciate the delicate subtleties. He put them down to the victim's diet, age, and to the actual melanin content of the eyes themselves.

One night he had just done away with a middle-aged woman, sucking her eyes out with his excising device, when a stray idea struck him.

How did he know that eyes were the best part of the human body to consume? Drusnev may have been eating them by the dozen, baked in pies, but that was the only evidence he had that eyes were the most stimulating to the taste-buds and the mind.

So, that night, Kaine took out a pocket-knife and carved away a portion of his victim's cheek. He didn't want to overdo it, just have a taste in case he was somehow missing out.

Once in the privacy of his apartment he ate the flesh, sprinkling it with a little paprika. It was not unpleasant, a little muscular and chewy, but with a definite meaty aftertaste.

As for euphoria, there was none of that.

No, no, Kaine thought to himself, as he sat down to a pair of attractive meadow-green eyes, he would be sticking to what he liked best.

Forty-seven

EACH DAY HE worked feverishly on a treatment for oculosis, as well as training other surgeons. Provided he got enough eyes — green eyes — he found that he was able to keep going without more than an hour or two of sleep.

The great delight was how each individual eye had a taste and texture unlike the last. Two eyes from the same pair were slightly different, too, complementing each other. Some eyes were nuttier than others, or had a subtle hint of spice. The most delicious were those of a hospital nurse that Kaine picked up on the Q-Line into Brooklyn. She was Hispanic and her eyes had a taste quite unlike anything else.

As for the worst — that was easy.

The surgeon had caught the eye of a middle-aged woman over in Queens — or rather, her eyes had caught his. They were deliciously green, almost unnatural in their hue. He had followed her through darkened streets, struck up a conversation, ended her life, and stuffed her body in a restaurant's waste bin.

Only later at home, as he scooped the first eye into his mouth, did he realize that she had been wearing coloured contact lenses.

Forty-eight

JUST AS HIS twelfth pair of prosthetic eyes was gone, the *New York Daily News* ran a front page exclusive. The headline ranted:

EYE-CRAZED SERIAL KILLER STALKS OUR STREETS!

If anything, Amadeus Kaine was rather disappointed by the article. It was all hype and no substance. They hadn't even worked out that the victims all shared the same eye colour.

Within an hour of reaching Mount Sinai that morning, the doctor was accosted by the fray of reporters who, until then, had been preoccupied with oculosis.

'Dr. Kaine, can you give a comment on the Eye Killer?' said a boisterous woman in black, a large microphone clutched tight in her left hand.

'Is that what they're calling him?'

The woman jerked a finger towards the microphone.

'Into this, please?'

'Look, in case you haven't noticed, we're pretty busy here,' said Kaine. 'Oculosis is mutating.'

'Mutating?'

'That's right.'

'D'you think it's got anything to do with the Eye Killer?' a reporter shouted from the back.

Amadeus Kaine scratched the back of his head incredulously.

'No, I don't,' he replied.

'Oh.'

Another reporter pushed forward.

'Could you tell us why someone would want to suck out the eyes of random people?'

The surgeon looked at him hard. He sensed his fingers trembling.

'I haven't got a clue,' he said.

Then the woman with the microphone pushed it forward again.

'One last question, doctor.'

'Sure.'

'The Eye Killer's victims all had glass eyes fitted.'

'Did they?'

'Yes. And I understand that glass eyes are pretty rare these days. There aren't many people in the US who can even make them.'

Kaine kept his cool.

'How do you know that the eyes fitted were new ones?'

The reporter shrugged.

As she did so, the surgeon smiled politely and slipped inside.

Forty-nine

HARRY J. MARRIS Jr. pressed his face up to the window of his office on the twenty-third floor of 26 Federal Plaza. He liked to watch the vehicles on Broadway stop-starting their way south, and to ponder about the lives of all the losers inside them.

As far as he was concerned, New York was an open-air asylum, a fact borne out by the current hysteria that someone down below was snapping people's necks and relieving them of their eyes.

In his twenty years with the FBI, Special Agent Marris had seen every kind of nutcase. He had seen psychopaths who stalked the aisles of Duane Reade, and schizophrenics who dressed up as Sleeping Beauty before killing old women walking their dogs. He had seen out-of-work actors who felt unbridled rage against anyone who gave them a bad review, and he had even seen a boxing promoter who went amok with a nail gun while dressed in a coat adorned in pretty pink feathers.

But the Eye Killer was unlike all the rest.

A team of ten agents under Marris was working on the profile, struggling to come up with a reason why anyone would target random people for their eyes. Three of them were devoted to tracing the last few makers of glass eyes.

As for motive, the best one they had come up with so far was that the killer bore a deep-seated grudge against an optician or an ophthalmologist. Beyond that, the team assumed there was a connection to oculosis, the buzzword of the age.

Special Agent Marris chaired the morning meeting, which began seven minutes late. He didn't much care for the so-called Eye Killer but, like everyone else in the room, he knew it was the chance of the decade — the chance to make a mark. With the cutbacks and bureau closures, nothing was so important as sticking out from the rank-and-file — and a serial killer with a difference was a good way of moving on up.

'Faulks, give us a breakdown on who he's preying on,' said Marris, almost bored by the question before it had emerged from his mouth.

'No significant profile's come out yet, sir. We've got pins all over the greater New York area.'

Agent Heather Matthews, a thirty-something hotshot newly sent up from Washington, held up a hand.

'If I may, sir?'

'Sure.'

'Well, I'd say he's a sexual deviant with massive physical strength and off-the-scale rage. I'm talking Incredible Hulk.'

'What about the link to oculosis? Does your Hulk have one?'

'I'm just spitballing here,' said Matthews, pushing back her hair, 'but I'm guessing he had the operation, and it went wrong.'

'So he's blind?'

'In one eye… just a guess.'

Marris dismissed the theory with a swish of his hand.

'Are you telling me that a half-blind Hulk can get glass eyes into position in the middle of the night?'

The team looked at the floor. They all disliked the Bureau chief shaming them with sarcasm.

'I'm guessing, sir, that he has a background in the ophthalmological world,' said Julius Listern studiously. Another upstart agent from DC, he was cutting his teeth on New York's psycho zone.

'What are you basing that on?'

'On the fact, sir, that he's inserting glass eyes so well.'

'Do you realize that you can get vintage glass eyes by the bucket load on eBay?' Marris barked. He looked out through the window, sighed hard, and then slowly turned his attention back to the room. 'Have any of you got the faintest idea what this psycho's doing with all these eyes?'

Agent Matthews held up her hand again.

'Eating them?' she said.

Even-tempered in the most stressful situations, Agent Marris thought of himself as the kind of chief that everyone liked. He didn't think much of the chiefs who made waves, because wave-makers always slipped up in the end. But once in a while someone said something that made his blood boil, because it was downright stupid. And the idea of a New Yorker — however deranged or downright Hulkish — eating the eyeballs of his fellow citizens, was just too much.

Agent Marris leapt to his feet, his face flushed with anger.

'You've just set a new record, Matthews!' he exclaimed. 'For the most cretinous remark of the week!'

Rooting his fingers through his thinning grey hair, Marris teaselled them back until they reached his neck.

'This may be the sickest society on the face of planet Earth,' he said angrily, 'but there's no way a New Yorker — however frigging deranged — would stoop to sucking out eyes and swallowing them!'

Fifty

THE ONLY SUBJECT on the agenda at Mount Sinai's Eye Department that morning was the mutation of viral oculosis. Kaine had agreed to chair a meeting of the senior ophthalmological staff. Before addressing them, he looked around the room. Everyone present was exhausted and dispirited, like warriors in a lost battle. He wished there was some way he could tell them about his real breakthrough, the breakthrough in the green eyes.

The more he thought of it, the more he came to see why cannibalism had been so prevalent throughout history. While the killing of humans might have been frowned upon, it had none of the taboo of cannibalism. It was something that Kaine couldn't understand. Surely it was far worse a crime to take a human life than to nibble a little human flesh?

Amadeus Kaine was seated in the middle of the long table, a mug of strong black coffee beside his right hand. When everyone was ready, he raised a finger.

Silence prevailed.

'Good morning to you all,' he said. 'I know we'd normally be conducting operations at this time, but I thought it important that we have a moment or two to reflect, to regroup.'

There was the howling sound of a siren out in the distance, a car crash victim being rushed through to emergency, but Kaine's concentration didn't falter.

'You will have heard about the Nebraskan mutation,' he said. 'It's alarming, and has occurred far more swiftly than I imagined. Yes, mutations are to be expected, but so quickly? It means either that oculosis has been dormant for longer than we realized, or that it is astonishingly progressive.'

'So what do we do, doctor?'

Kaine looked to his left. The voice had come from a young woman whom he didn't recognize. He frowned.

'I'm Dr. Alexa Hodge, seconded to Mount Sinai from Miami,' she said, as if answering his question.

'Welcome, Dr. Hodge,' Kaine replied. 'And to answer your question, we try to work out the natural pathology — what it's gonna do next.'

'It's gonna plunge us all into a void of darkness,' said a surgeon at the far end of the table. 'You don't need to be a genius to work that one out.'

Amadeus Kaine leaned forward on his knuckles.

'I disagree with you, Dr. Upton,' he said. 'I believe we can out-think oculosis, that we can beat it. But in order to do so, we have to learn to think in new ways — in ways no human has ever thought before.'

'And you've got a magic pill to change the way we all think?'

Kaine allowed his stern expression to melt into a smile.

'I wish that I had, doctor,' he said, 'but even if I did, I expect it wouldn't be legal.'

Forty minutes later, the meeting was over and the staff filed out fast. There was no time to waste in loitering.

As Kaine was carefully sliding his paperwork into a calfskin attaché case, Alexa Hodge approached.

'Can I ask what your thoughts are on the Eye Killer, doctor?' she asked.

Kaine looked up slowly and felt his brow warming.

'You mean the whacko who's killing people for their eyes?'

'The very same.'

'Well, I assume there's some link to oculosis. Maybe someone's doing some do-it-yourself research?' He smiled. 'A joke,' he added.

'But why would they need to kill, when they could just knock over an eye bank?' Dr. Hodge grinned. 'A joke.'

'Huh?' said Kaine. He wiped a hand down over his face, stunned that he hadn't thought of it himself.

'You OK, doctor?'

'Yes, yes, sorry. My mind's a million miles away,' the surgeon said.

Fifty-one

THE NEXT AFTERNOON, a plastic container the size and shape of a cooler arrived. Amadeus Kaine was waiting for it at the door. He signed, then slipped the guy from FedEx a tip. Never had he awaited a delivery with such unbridled anticipation.

The container was marked with all the usual stickers stating the urgency of the contents, and it was only there at all because Kaine was who he was. The nation's leading eye surgeon could request certain perks without eliciting any questions.

And one of the best perks imaginable was having a dozen prime green eyes shipped over to him from the eminent Minnesota Lions Eye Bank in Saint Paul.

Dr. Kaine carried the container through to his laboratory and opened it up. He waded through the layers of packaging, removed the cooling element, and got down to the vials. His body was tingling with anticipation.

There was no need to kill ever again.

The best thing of all — even better than not having to take another life — was the fact that the eyes could be ordered by colour, and that they came direct to his door for free. No matter how many eyes he ordered, or what colour they were, no one would suspect anything at all.

Opening up the first vial, Kaine tipped out the contents onto his palm. It was a good, firm eye, a little cold, but of the highest quality. The iris was jade green. As he considered it sitting in his hand, the surgeon found it appealing not knowing whose face it had come from. After all, the last thing one wants to know when choosing a steak is what the animal's face looked like.

But the eye hadn't come from an animal. It was human — a point that filled Dr. Kaine with bizarre excitement. He couldn't explain it, but felt certain that eye-eating would catch on if other people just had the chance to indulge in the rare cuisine. Yes, it was a forbidden fruit, but it was a fruit so delicious, and with such an impact on the mental faculties, that there was no question about the merits of devouring it. In the same way that we all try to forget where caviar comes from, the surgeon believed people would make an exception when it came to fresh human eyes.

Sticking out his tongue, he placed the jade-green eyeball upon it, and retracted it slowly into his mouth.

The next fifteen seconds were sheer bliss.

The eye had a hint of sage, a consistency a little firmer than those of his recent New York conquests. Kaine chewed very slowly, allowing the juices to be mixed in with his saliva. As the eye moved around the warm confines of his mouth, he played the first movement of Elgar's Cello Concerto in his mind.

When the eyeball had been swallowed, his fingers reached for another. There was all the temptation of a chocolate box. He cursed himself, and tut-tutted. If he were to out-think oculosis, he would need to ration them.

He laughed out loud.

But why the need for rationing, when he could order as many as he liked? Pulling back the lid of the package, Kaine dug in his hand and tapped out another eye. A moment later it, too, was heading down towards his stomach.

Fifty-two

FOR SEVEN DAYS Harry Marris pored over the Eye Killer evidence, and he requested ten more agents to be assigned to the case. There may have been panic on the streets of New York, but the oculosis epidemic had already shaken society to the point of mania.

A great many ordinary people were barricaded up at home, ordering everything they needed online. Cyber retailers levied huge premiums for making deliveries in such adverse conditions, but in New York and elsewhere people paid up rather than venture outside. Children were home-schooled, employees cut work, and restaurants and public places were shunned.

Each day, it seemed, another myth surrounding the virus became ingrained in society. Some people claimed that oculosis could be treated by washing one's eyes in a mixture of Coca-Cola and boiled milk, or that smearing the entire head with petroleum jelly was effective in keeping the symptoms at bay. One treatment from Los Angeles — supposedly used by Hollywood stars, no less — involved breathing helium for ten minutes each morning through a special respiration device.

Agent Marris knew that each of the victims he discovered increased his chance of catching the Eye Killer. Disapproving of speculation, he liked to piece the evidence together bit by bit. And the evidence pointed clearly to a man with both surgical training and impressive upper body strength. As for his hunch, Marris felt certain the killer was motivated by a grievance of some kind, a grievance against people with green eyes.

But all of a sudden, the trail had gone cold.

Special Agent Marris couldn't understand it. Why wasn't the Eye Killer striking any more? He had been killing as regular as clockwork.

Then, suddenly — nothing.

Perhaps he had himself gone down with oculosis, or had been wounded while launching an attack.

The Bureau chief shook his head at his own speculations. No, no, there had to be a simpler reason. He could feel it in his gut.

It was obvious.

The Eye Killer wasn't killing because another opportunity had presented itself.

Fifty-three

A FEW MILES away, on the Upper East Side, Amadeus Kaine signed for another FedEx delivery. Using his contacts and high-flying reputation, he had acquired ninety-nine more eyes for scientific research from an eye bank in Chicago. There was no point in messing around with smaller quantities. And, besides, Kaine liked multiples of three.

Seventy of them were green, ranging in colour from lime to a darker avocado green. The remaining specimens were blue, brown, and grey. He had asked for as many green eyes as possible, justifying the request by hinting at a link between melanin and oculosis.

No longer requiring sleep, he conducted experiments and tests all night, every night. Sometimes he would have a bowl of eyes on hand in the lab and snack on them as though they were salted peanuts. When more relaxed, he would make a ceremony of it, serving them up nicely with truffle oil or a few drops of aged balsamic vinegar from a prized source in Modena.

At the eye banks themselves there was a sense of satisfaction that they had been of some small service to the most celebrated of surgeons. In their view, Kaine was the one man alive believed to have real hope of combating the scourge of viral oculosis.

As word of the doctor's experiments spread, eye banks far and wide began sending supplies without even being asked to do so. They saw it as an altruistic gesture in a time of national emergency.

As a result, the refrigerator at the surgeon's home was stacked with trays of human eyes, as was the freezer. There were hundreds more packed into the fridge in his lab. Whereas he'd savoured the eyes like a true delicacy when he was murdering for them, Kaine had become relatively nonchalant. Guzzling them by the handful, he hardly gave a thought to eating them.

Two weeks after the first eye bank delivery, Kaine was consuming around forty eyes a day. Any more than that and he felt queasy, as if over-indulging on foie gras. Having experimented with every conceivable colour, he settled on emerald green as his very favourite. There were hidden layers of depth to the taste, mixed with a subtlety in texture that only an eye-eating connoisseur would have understood. More importantly, though, the green eyes offered a kind of prophetic sense of knowledge, one that was far less evident in any other colour.

But the more eyes Kaine ate, the less of a rush he got.

The point came at which two-dozen eyes gave the same hit as a single one had in the early days, the days of his hasty retreat from West Africa.

It was not true to say that Kaine felt entirely innocent. He knew very well that the habit was wayward, and he tried time and again to cut down. He made promises to himself, vowing to mend his ways. But, now an expert on the nature of addiction, he knew that it was far too late to stop.

The point came at which he wasn't eating anything else. By now he laughed at the idea of obscure cuisines, the kind that used to titillate his friends, dismissing them as a juvenile foible.

Human eyes were the only obscure food worth bothering with. Devoting hours to considering the subject, he didn't see why they had to be regarded as so illicit and obscure. If he could have had his way, everyone would have been dining on nice fresh eyes and nothing else.

A pulse of electricity suddenly ran down the surgeon's spine. Thank God they weren't consumed by the masses, though, he thought. Because if they were, then there would be shortages and price hikes. He may have been living on a cuisine that horrified everyone else, but the fact that he alone was eating them meant that there were all the more for him.

Fifty-four

In the third week of February, Special Agent Marris made a breakthrough of his own. Forensic testing on Marcie Williamson's ocular cavities had revealed a DNA trace. There was no match on CODIS, but that just meant the attacker didn't have a record. Additional tests on the other cadavers robbed of their eyes suggested that a machine of some description had been used.

Within a day or so, Marris had matched the particular marks with those presented by the so-called Kaine Excisor. The next stage was to check every licensed Excisor. The majority had been sold to hospitals around the United States. A few were in use overseas, most of them in Britain and Scandinavia. There were more than three thousand in total, the greatest number of all in the New York municipal area.

The FBI had been lent one of the machines. Agent Marris had placed it on his desk. He was fascinated by it, intrigued by the thought of anyone dreaming up such a device.

'Who the hell came up with it?' he wondered aloud in a meeting the next morning.

'An eye surgeon… Doctor Amadeus B. Kaine.'

'Who's he?'

Agent Spitz held up a printout from Wikipedia.

'In the world of ophthalmology, he's as close as there is to a god.'

'*Meaning?*'

'Meaning that he's a leader in his field — the one surgeon alive who could possibly ever come up with an answer to oculosis.'

'Which hospital is he affiliated with?'

Special Agent Cleaves glanced at his notes.

'With Mount Sinai, sir, although he works with a number of others, including the New York Presbyterian.'

'Has he got an office?'

'654 Madison Avenue,' said Agents Spitz and Cleaves at the same time.

'What I'm thinking is that I need to get in the head of someone who can use one of these Excisor things,' said Marris. 'One of you get me an appointment with this ophthalmological god.'

Fifty-five

'THE OCULOSIS ISSUE has been wearing us all down,' said Kaine, as he led Special Agent Marris through to his office. 'I've closed my regular practice for the moment and am working around the clock on finding a cure.'

'I hear you're the man who can do it — if anyone can,' said Marris hopefully. He looked into the surgeon's eyes and saw a man of brilliance, a man with secrets. And Kaine looked at the special agent, taking in his mint-green eyes. He sensed his mouth water ever so slightly.

'Please, have a seat, Agent...'

'Marris. Like Harris but with an M.'

'Got it. What can I do for you?'

'I understand you invented a kind of machine, called the Kaine...'

'Excisor.'

'Right, yes. That's it.' The FBI man let out a laugh. 'I'd like to see inside your head,' he said.

'And why is that?'

'Well, it's complicated, isn't it?'

Kaine smoothed a hand down the sleeve of his jacket. It was Merino wool, woven in Rome and cut at Huntsman on London's Savile Row.

'In eye surgery most things are complicated,' he replied.

'And a machine like your Excisor, do you need special training to work a thing like that?'

'Well, I suppose a little background on the human eye would come in handy.'

'How long does it take?'

'Excuse me?'

'To cut out an eye? How long does the Excisor take?'

'Oh, about five minutes, if done right.'

'Each eye?'

'We usually only excise one.'

'Always?'

Kaine sniffed. He touched a finger to his left nostril.

'Usually,' he repeated. He paused, looked at the special agent again, and wondered how he might encourage him to leave. 'I imagine you are enquiring about the so-called Eye Killer,' he said.

'That's right. He's been using a device similar to yours.'

'How interesting.' Kaine smiled. 'He has impeccable taste then.'

Marris stood up and crossed the room, walking over to the Atmos clock.

'You've got some nice stuff.'

'Thank you.'

'I'm guessing, what... you're on six figures, a man like you.' The surgeon frowned. He wanted to be left alone so that he could have a little snack.

'I am one of those people who likes to collect but never has an idea of how much they have,' he said blankly.

Marris stepped over to the small panelled door at the end of the room.

'And where does this lead?' he asked.

'Oh, just to my laboratory.'

'Would you mind if I poked my head inside? I used to love science at school.'

'Yes of course. Go right in.'

Agent Marris disappeared into the lab. Kaine didn't follow him. He didn't want to be lured into a tug-of-war of questioning.

There was silence for a minute and a half, and Marris' head came round the door.

'Would you mind coming in here for a moment, doctor?' he asked.

Kaine stepped through, bracing himself for a volley of questions he would have preferred not to answer.

'Yes?'

'These cartons stacked up here... they look like they were shipped here recently.'

'That's right, they were.'

'And what did they contain exactly?'

'Eyes. Human eyes.'

Special Agent Marris touched the tip of his tongue to his upper lip.

'*Eyes?*'

'That's right,' said Kaine. 'As you'll remember, I'm an eye surgeon.'

'And where did they come from, these eyes?'

'From eye banks, mostly. You see, I'm doing exhaustive tests on oculosis. And I think I'm nearing a major breakthrough. It's been a battle, but I'm damned if we're gonna lose.'

Marris managed a phony smile of congratulation.

'I'm in the presence of greatness,' he said.

'I don't know about that.'

'Well, everyone speaks of you very highly.'

'How good of them.'

Agent Marris wanted to ask something but wasn't quite sure what.

'I'm a little confused,' he said, after a long silence.

'About what?'

'About why a brilliant surgeon like you doesn't have dozens of people working for him.'

'People?'

'You know — interns, assistants, other scientists... a receptionist.'

Kaine grinned.

'People like that just get in the way. Believe me, I speak from experience.'

'So you're a loner?'

'I wouldn't say that. I have colleagues at Mount Sinai, and other hospitals.'

'And friends?'

'Yes, I have friends.' Kaine held up a hand, then swallowed. 'I don't understand where you're going with this,' he said.

Special Agent Marris pulled open the refrigerator door and peeked inside, taking in the gruesome contents of a large, clear plastic tub.

'Eyes?' he asked quizzically.

'That's right.'

'I guess I should be surprised to find anything else.'

'Well, as I said, I am an eye surgeon.'

The FBI agent paced back through to the office. He glanced at the clock again, more because he appreciated the Jaeger workmanship than from a need to know the time.

Just as he was about to go through again to the reception, something caught his eye.

It was on a low table to the right of the clock.

A bowl with a silver soup spoon in it.

And on the spoon was a blue human eye.

Marris was unshockable. The ability to show no excitement and to remain calm was a cornerstone of FBI training. But Dr. Kaine was pushing his unshockability to the limit.

He turned faster than he would have liked, glancing down at the carpet.

'I'm grateful to you, doctor,' he said. 'I'm sure we'll meet again.'

Kaine smiled absently. He went back into his office and checked his wristwatch against the Jaeger Atmos clock.

Then he spooned the eyeball onto his tongue and swallowed it whole.

Fifty-six

WITHIN THIRTY-FIVE MINUTES, 654 Madison Avenue had been staked out like no building had ever been staked out before. Every five feet an armed officer was in position, with a Mobile Command Center dug in at the far end of the block.

Pedestrians were being moved away, channelled through to surrounding streets. The Calvin Klein store on the ground floor was being emptied of its customers by uniformed officers from NYPD. And, next door, in the foyer of No. 654's office building, a SWAT team was checking for explosives, with another making its way up to the roof.

In his office, Kaine was finishing a second bowl of eyes, while scribbling down a theory on viral mutation that had just come to him. In a flash of inspiration, he had made a connection between the poultry vector of oculosis and the spread of foot and mouth disease a decade earlier. The similarities allowed the surgeon to anticipate arcs of progression in mutation — a key factor in establishing an inoculation for the oculosis pandemic.

He stood up, turned to the window, and rocked back and forth on his heels. In the background, the Jaeger clock marked the seconds delicately, forming a backbone of structure and reliability to the afternoon. Closing his eyes, Amadeus Kaine drank in the movement through his ears. The Swiss, he thought to himself, there was no race like them.

If he had his way everyone would be like the Swiss.

Opening his eyes, he glanced down at the ant-people on Madison Avenue. He was about to feel pity for them, as he always did. But for the first time in all the years he had been staring down in pity, there weren't any ant-people to pity. Even with oculosis crippling the city, there were usually still a few commuters out there.

Strange, he thought.

Allowing his gaze to move along the length of the street as far as the corner of 61st Street, he scoured the pavement. There wasn't a suited ant in sight. But there were police. Hundreds of them.

A twisted pang of apprehension shot down the surgeon's spine.

Marris.

He knew the agent had picked up on something.

Without wasting a moment, Kaine grabbed an aluminium wheelie case from the corner. It was made in Germany by Rimowa and was of a size that always passed for hand luggage. Dumping out the papers and files, he went through to the lab. Once there, he opened the fridge and poured the eyes into a soft cooler bag before placing it in the case.

Then, charging back into the office, he picked up his attaché case from beneath his desk. Checking his passport was inside, he opened a drawer and took out ten identical manila envelopes. The first contained five diplomatic passports — a perk from doing business with the iniquitous leaders of dictatorships. The other nine were filled with wads of crisp 500-euro notes, each one an inch thick. Kaine tossed them into the aluminium case and clicked it shut.

Then he picked up another case. It was smaller than the first.

But, before running out of the door, he walked calmly over to the Atmos clock and gave it a kiss.

Two minutes later, the SWAT team burst in.

They moved in formation through the reception, the office, the laboratory and adjoining rooms. In full combat armour, they had their weapons raised to eye level.

'He's gone, sir!' yelled one of the team.

'Secure the area! And get aerial support to check the roof!'

A minute later, Special Agent Marris hurried in.

'*And...?*'

'And the bird has flown the coop.'

'Damn it!'

'Don't worry, sir,' said the SWAT leader. 'There's no way in hell he can get past us. We've got all exits covered.'

Agent Marris went over to the desk. He scanned its surface, taking in the photographs with world leaders and celebrities, the awards and the assortment of fine writing instruments. He picked up the gold-plated orb from its wooden stand and read the name 'Bhochnivia' on the side, his lips sounding out the syllables.

He frowned, closed his eyes, and shouted:

'I want Kaine's face pasted up at every port and airport and on the Most Wanted list within the hour!'

Fifty-seven

THIRTY MINUTES LATER, six military Humvees in graphite grey swept fast up Madison Avenue, sirens blaring and lights ablaze. The doors of each were marked with biohazard symbols. As soon as they had pulled to a halt outside number 654, the biohazard response team clambered down, half a dozen officers in each vehicle. They were dressed in positive pressure personnel suits with full face masks and breathing packs.

Their leader, Lieutenant Forester, motioned a hand to the building.

'Unit One, secure the perimeter! Unit Two, secure the basement! Unit Three, take the elevator shafts! Unit Four, you're with me!'

Forester charged into the foyer, the rubber soles of his one-piece uniform stepping silently across the marble in the direction of the elevators.

Agent Spitz cut him off before he reached them.

'Can I help you?' she said, confused.

'Lieutenant Forester of the Biohazard Response Team from Fort Bragg. We've had a Level 4 breach called in, something about it being related to oculosis. Cutting-edge research.'

'A breach of what?'

'Marburg virus, ma'am.'

'The FBI has had no information on this.'

'A 911 call at…' Forester checked the note on his tablet, 'less than an hour ago.'

'Well, we've got a murder suspect in the building.'

'Armed with?'

Special Agent Spitz took a step back.

'He breaks his victims' necks,' she said.

Lieutenant Forester held up his palm to silence her.

'Biohazard trumps bare hands,' he replied.

Striding over to the left elevator, he took it to the top floor.

Agent Spitz reported the arrival of the Biohazard Response Team into her radio. There was a short delay, and Marris's furious voice broke through the static.

'Get them the hell out of here!'

'But, sir, they say there's been a biohazard called in.'

'What frigging biohazard?'

'Mar… Mar-bot… Marbol… Marburg… that's it, Marburg virus, sir.'

'What?!'

'They're saying it's a Level 4 breach.'

'Where the hell are they?'

'They're on their way up.'

Fifty-eight

IN HIS YOUTH, Amadeus Kaine had read an account of a Holocaust survivor who had managed to keep the family jewels from the Nazis by putting them in the least obvious place — in the middle of the kitchen table, covered by a folded newspaper. The Brownshirts had ransacked the entire house but never checked under the newspaper.

It was a lesson Kaine had always remembered.

With the might of the FBI bearing down on him, he wondered what the Holocaust survivor with the folded newspaper would have done. The answer is that he would have remained calm and done something no one could have expected.

Taking the stairs to the ninth floor, Kaine had found a public washroom to the right of the elevator. Stepping into the female toilet, he had unpacked the biohazard suit and put it on. The American Biological Safety Association had lent it to him when he was called out to a hazardous waste depot in Guam. For weeks the surgeon had cursed them for failing to collect it. As he donned the suit, he had said a prayer of thanks for inefficiencies, most notably of dear Mrs. Phelps.

Before slipping the respiration visor down, he had transferred his clothing and the contents of the aluminium case into the one in which the suit had been packed. The exterior was covered in biohazard symbols. Before clicking it shut, he had removed a nice green eye from the stock and gulped it down.

Fifty-nine

FIVE MINUTES LATER, Kaine was in a taxi heading upstate.

He changed back into his regular clothes, then sprawled out on the rear seat. It was a long journey, one which gave him time to consider his next steps. After a little snooze, he reserved a private jet using his iPad. The firm was popular with celebrities, who appreciated their discretion. It was used to the fickle whims and the security needs of the jetset, and didn't require an actual destination until moments before takeoff.

As for the rendezvous point, Kaine had chosen the Tompkins Regional Airport outside Ithaca. It was the one access point he could be certain the Feds wouldn't have under their watchful gaze.

Stretching back, Kaine yawned a yawn of supreme confidence. That was the problem with the secret service — they never covered all their bases.

Having drifted off to sleep again for a little while, he had a snack and, re-energized by it, coaxed himself to think hard. There were all kinds of choices. A host of dictators would, for instance, have appreciated seeing him again. For years he had made a speciality of treating them and their families. The only drawback with tin-pot dictators was that their luck tended to run out just when they needed it most — a kind of natural expiration date.

But there were so many of them that there were plenty to choose from.

What about Damascus? Kaine thought. He was fond of the architecture in the old city, especially the Umayyad Mosque, and its dictator Bashar al-Assad was not only a personal friend but an eye surgeon as well. Amadeus Kaine dismissed the idea. No, no, Assad's days seemed numbered now, although he himself hadn't recognized it.

He thought again.

What about West Africa? There was an abundance of first-rate despots there clinging to power, each one twice as degenerate as the last.

Suddenly, an idea began to form itself in the surgeon's mind.

The moment he thought of it he knew it was the right choice.

Istanbul.

He would go to Istanbul. Why? He loved the early Ottoman architecture, the food, the culture, and the vibrant hybrid of Oriental and Occidental style.

But that was not why he selected it.

The reason was that Istanbul, crossroads of East and West, was home to more people with green eyes than anywhere else on Earth.

Sixty

654 MADISON AVENUE was swept and swept again for biohazard, bombs, ballistics, and for a wayward surgeon with a case full of human eyes. For more than a day and a

half Special Agent Marris combed the place, mapping out the ventilation ducts, the elevator shafts and the storage areas in which a fugitive could have dug down.

In his gut he knew he wouldn't find Kaine there, that the surgeon must have absconded long before. Following FBI protocol, he had his team go through every corner of Kaine's life, from the toothpaste he used to the dusty shoebox under his bed.

It was filled with snow globes the doctor had collected as a child.

Sixty-one

OVER THE DAYS that followed, the Feds interviewed anyone they could find who had known Amadeus Kaine, either in a professional capacity or in his private circle.

They spoke to fellow surgeons and to hospital staff — all of whom raved about a man regarded as decades ahead of his time. They spoke to the members of the Obscure Cuisine Dining Club, and heard from them that Kaine had been an exemplary member, the kind of man who took obscure dining to new heights. And they spoke to William McMarsh, and learned that the celebrated eye surgeon had been married to a woman named Francine.

'Where is she now?' asked the interviewing officer.

'Still up in Vermont, I guess.'

'Who divorced who?'

'He divorced her.'

'Why?'

'She had an affair with his best friend. Well, that was just the start of it.'

'D'you know if they ever speak?'

McMarsh grinned.

'Are you crazy? He calls her the Antichrist.'

'What colour eyes did she have?'

The butcher shrugged.

'Can't quite remember,' he said.

Sixty-two

SEATED IN A patch of yellow morning light in a garden, Dr. Kaine looked out towards the Bosphorus, and thanked his good fortune.

Over the years of his meteoric career, Istanbul was a place that had provided refuge time and again. No other city on Earth enthralled him as it did. He loved the grandeur of it all, the mystery, and the sense of power, and the way that one city could bridge two continents. But, above all, he adored how it sucked you in and protected you from the outside world. He might have previously sought its shelter against the limelight of celebrity, but Amadeus Kaine had not travelled there as a fugitive before.

Peering out at an oil tanker cruising the sapphire waters below the little villa he had rented, he let out a shrill laugh. It may have been a grave moment, but the surgeon found it decidedly amusing. That damn Agent

Marris, he thought, he couldn't trap a rubber duck in a bath of tepid water. Was he really the best the Feds could come up with?

Kaine picked a mobile phone from the wrought-iron table before him and dialled a number from memory. It began 0041-44 — the dialling code for Zurich.

'Christian, hello my friend, it's Amadeus Kaine,' he said with a smile.

There was a pause.

'Dr. Kaine, good to hear your voice.'

'I have been dealing with a matter of discretion, Christian. I'd be grateful to have some funds wired to me at your earliest convenience.'

'Of course,' replied the voice. 'The usual arrangement?'

'That's just what I had in mind. No paper trail. If you have a pencil ready I'll give you the details now.'

Kaine dictated a series of numbers, followed by an amount — three million US dollars. He thanked his manager at AKB Privatbank, and placed the telephone back on the table, his fingers tracing the curled iron leg as he did so.

After that, he went online and ordered a comprehensive array of medical equipment and supplies, most of them from Riester Medical and a variety of other Swiss firms. The inventory was enough to service a hospital's entire ophthalmological department.

When he had placed the order, the eye surgeon slumped back in the chair. He thought about Francine, his ex-wife, and what she would tell the Feds when they tracked her down. She would surely delight in dreaming up all manner of psychopathic details for their notebooks.

For lunch he grilled some calamari marinated in garlic and lemon juice. Then, with the winter shadows lengthening, he took a stroll. It was a long one, all the way from Bebek to a building in Sultanahmet. Clutched in his hand was a scrap of paper, with an address written out in neat capital letters.

He arrived outside just as it was closing up for the night. It didn't worry him, as he hadn't planned to go inside. Instead, he watched from a discreet distance.

A man came out, put on his hat, and walked off in the opposite direction. Then a woman left. She got into a van and drove away. The vehicle had a symbol on the side, the same one as was displayed above the building.

Large and blue, it was in the shape of a human eye.

Sixty-three

WITH KAINE NO longer leading the ophthalmological scene, the battle against oculosis quickly disintegrated. Despite using the disgraced surgeon's technique, other specialists discovered that the disease had mutated again, this time with a terrible new twist.

It had suddenly and inexplicably become airborne.

At FBI Headquarters in Washington, the Emergency Medical Crisis Unit convened. All the relevant department chiefs were summoned. Agent Marris was there too, by special invitation. After all, he had been the one who had let Kaine get away — thereby limiting the chances of finding a real cure.

Thomas W. Griff, Director of the FBI, knocked a knuckle on the conference table. His face was lined with worry. He hadn't slept well in days.

'Here's the understatement of the week,' he said in a cold, rancorous voice. 'Oculosis is getting out of hand. It's one genie I wish we could stuff back into the bottle.'

Special Advisor Ralph Zuicker waved a pencil raised in line with his ear.

'Excuse me for speaking out,' he said, 'but even if we caught Dr. Amadeus Kaine, we could hardly allow him to continue his research, could we?'

'But he was the one man who could provide real hope,' said an agent to Zuicker's left.

'He led the field,' added another.

'So?'

Ralph Zuicker shrugged.

'So what, sir?'

Griff wove his fingers together.

'So you're saying that we track down the guy who could save the sight of our entire species and throw him into the deepest dungeon we've got?'

'He's made us a laughing stock,' said Marris angrily. 'And he has to pay for that.'

The director rolled his eyes.

'Right now, I'd laugh along with everyone else,' he said, 'if we could get an inoculation against the virus. And from where I'm sitting Kaine's our only hope.'

'What leads do we have?' asked Zuicker.

Agent Marris cleared his throat.

'His ex-wife said she thought he'd have gone to Park City, that he liked it there.'

'I bet he's still in New York,' Griff replied. 'The smartest guys always stay safe, and safe means a place they know.'

'He took a bunch of eyes with him,' said Marris.

'Huh?'

'Eyes. He took a whole case of them. I saw them in his fridge, the one in the lab.'

'How many were there?'

'A couple hundred I'd say. All swishing around, they were. It was pretty gross.'

The director held out a hand.

'I want every agent in this nation searching for Amadeus Kaine,' he said. 'And while you're at it, get the CIA onto him as well. I promise you he'll surface. Grade-A lunatics like that always do. It's just a question of time.'

Sixty-four

THREE DELIVERY TRUCKS pulled up at the small villa Kaine had rented in Bebek. The lead driver assumed he had been sent to the wrong address. He checked it over the radio. The details were confirmed, and so he rang the bell.

There was a long pause and then Dr. Kaine opened the door. He was wearing a plaid bathrobe and a pair of suede slippers.

'A special delivery from Switzerland,' the driver said, as he glanced down at the clipboard. 'In the name of Mr. Victor Oskovich.'

'That's me,' said Kaine. 'Bring it all in.'

Later that day, he heard from a barber that the Turkish authorities were rounding up anyone suffering from oculosis and had begun treating them at a small unit on the outskirts of Istanbul. It seemed that there was terrible shame associated with the disease.

'They get it because they like McDonald's,' the barber had said. 'Filet-O-Fish gives you the sickness in the left eye, and Big Macs in the right eye.'

'Are you sure?' Kaine had asked, dubiously.

'Believe me, sir, I speak the truth.'

The same afternoon, the eye surgeon took a taxi from his villa to the clinic that the barber had mentioned — Clinic Samsun.

It was a dingy place, with thin walls, filthy nylon curtains, and a sense of utter dread. There were patients everywhere. The lucky ones were lying on beds, or were seated in rigid old school chairs. The rest of them were crouching on the ground, or propped up against the windows.

They all had bandaged eyes.

In his jacket pocket, Kaine had a Belarusian passport in the name of Victor Oskovich. The country's dictator, Alexander Lukashenko, had presented it to Kaine himself three years before. As with his other foreign passports, Kaine had requested a new identity, as a kind of joke. He never expected that they would actually be useful.

Ten minutes after arriving at Clinic Samsun, the American had been welcomed by the director, a burly physician from Anatolia, called Dr. Evren. He didn't seem in the least surprised that a foreign surgeon would turn up and start dispensing advice.

'We get more and more cases all the time,' the director said, 'but we don't know what to do. There's no cure, as you know.'

Dr. Kaine asked to see the newest patient. He was taken to a child of about ten, a boy, whose eyesight was already lost. Having made a brief examination of the child, Kaine was taken to the operating theatre.

'I can help,' he said.

The director seemed pleased, but perplexed.

'The boy... you can help the boy?'

'I can help them all,' he said.

Sixty-five

THREE WEEKS AFTER Amadeus Kaine's escape from Madison Avenue, the military were called in to protect the citizens of New York. With blindness now affecting tens of thousands of ordinary people from coast to coast, society had all but completely broken down. Hysteria had set in, and most citizens never went out, except in a desperate search for food and basic supplies. When they did leave their homes, they wore swimming goggles or ski masks, and wrapped scarves tight over their mouths.

There was almost nothing to buy. Most of the supermarkets and food stores were shuttered up. Many more had been looted or razed to the ground.

As for online retailers, they had all ceased to function as well, a knock-on effect from the fact their employees were either blind or unable to get in to work. Without the personnel to drive the trains or buses, or to monitor the traffic lights, the entire transportation system had ground to a halt.

Muggings and robberies were so frequent that the police had given up trying to investigate any that were reported. The hospitals had no way of coping with the constant stream of patients, most of whom were now afflicted with oculosis in both eyes.

Mobile field hospitals had been set up on the north and south ends of Central Park, and down near Wall Street, too. But their teams had no training to combat the constantly mutating disease. There were scenes of panic, and of demonstrations. Government buildings were targeted, although the majority were quite empty as most employees had no way to get to work.

In any case, those who could see were fleeing from the municipal area. Some of them drove, and quickly found themselves mired in gridlock, with a great many more simply travelling on foot.

Taking with them all they could carry, their desperate hope was of reaching a corner of the country where oculosis had not yet prevailed. But New York's devastation was enacted in every city and town in the nation.

Agent Marris felt a deep hatred towards nature when, one morning, his ten-year-old son woke up blind. His wife broke down in tears, ripping out her hair, blaming her husband for not capturing the one man alive who could have made a difference.

Sixty-six

IN THE CRISIS bunker deep beneath Pennsylvania Avenue, Director Griff called a special meeting to order. His face was drawn, his expression even more sour than usual.

'I'm not going to waste your time or my own with pleasantries,' he said. 'From today onwards the FBI will be working with the military in a joint effort to restore a basic functionality to our nation's urban landscape.'

Seated opposite Griff was a stern-looking woman in a tailored wool suit. Her greying hair was tied back in a small bun, her manner cold and decidedly aggressive. Her name was Dr. Ella Raush, and she was the special liaison, answering directly to the president.

Signalling to Griff, she cut in:

'With respect, Director, I think it's clear to say that there's no hope in hell of establishing anything near to "normality" any time soon. The president has asked me to say that any resources will be made available to quash oculosis.' She paused, drew breath, and said: 'And, he has asked me to request that you find Dr. Amadeus Kaine at any cost.'

'Kaine's disappeared,' Griff replied.

'Where to?'

The director shrugged.

'No one knows… he's disappeared. That's the point.'

'He may even be blind himself,' said a senior member of Griff's staff. 'It's just a theory we're working on.'

'Or he could be in Timbuktu for all we know,' another whispered.

Dr. Raush removed her glasses and laid them gently on the desk. She wanted Griff and the others to see her expression without any interference of glass.

'I don't imagine that I have to remind you all,' she said in an icy tone, 'that we have at our fingertips the most sophisticated network of surveillance in the history of the planet. Surely it's not so hard to find the inimitable Dr. Kaine.'

Sixty-seven

THE THREE BEDROOMS of the Bebek villa had been transformed into makeshift laboratories, with the large sitting room providing additional space for extra equipment. In the back garden the doctor had installed a chicken coop with fifty birds, each one a different variety.

Working all day and all night, every night, on his cure for oculosis, his improvised lab was better geared to enabling him to understand the disease than any other on Earth.

Without distraction, and with his mind nourished by the supply of American eyes he had brought with him, Kaine found he was able to complete a year's research in a matter of days. The only problem was that the contents of the box in his fridge were running low.

There were only five eyes left.

The surgeon may have been a fugitive, and a murderer, but he really didn't want to take a human life again. He wasn't a cold-blooded killer, not like the kind you found on death row or featured in the nightly news. His terminations were, as he saw it, a means to an end, a method by which his mind could be stimulated and freed.

From the moment he had arrived in Turkey, he had been amazed by the sheer quantity of green eyes. They were everywhere — in the faces of taxi drivers and housewives, commuters, shop assistants and policemen. Even his landlord had green eyes — a particularly striking shade of olive. And it was as if the entire culture was obsessed with eyes or, rather, the Evil Eye. Glass talismans to avert its malevolent power hung in every car, office, and home.

Taking a break from his experiments, Kaine considered whether he ought to start killing again once the last of the eyes had been consumed. He quickly dismissed the idea. No, no, far better to pay a visit to the eye bank and make a withdrawal. Simply asking for a donation was one possibility. On second thoughts, Kaine dismissed that, too. After all, his alias, Dr. Victor Oskovich, had no international reputation. No one would have given him the time of day.

After another full night of experimentation, the doctor stepped out onto the terrace and watched the sun rise above

Istanbul. He had witnessed many marvellous things in his life, but dawn over what was once Constantinople sent a shiver down his spine.

It was a sight to cherish.

As he stared at it, the rays of faint orange light were diffused by the boiling tapestry of cloud, tinges of violet and pale blue. There was an ethereal quality, as though it were somehow above anything else conjured by nature.

Kaine rubbed his eyes. They were itching from all the experiments, the lack of sleep, and from staring down into a microscope day after day.

He needed a rest.

Pacing through into the bathroom, he soaked a cloth in warm water and pressed it to his face. The itching turned to burning. Too wound up to sleep, and with the pain increasing, Kaine took half a sleeping pill and promised not to drive himself as furiously from then on. He lay down on the old mahogany bedstead and slowly drifted into sleep.

When he awoke, six hours later, he was blind.

Sixty-eight

EVERY CIA BUREAU and sub-bureau on the planet had been sent a briefing about Dr. Amadeus Kaine. It consisted of a photograph taken from his Mount Sinai ID, together with a fleeting description of his life and work.

He was described as having a fascination for 'obscure foods' as well as being an Anglophile. As a leading ophthalmological surgeon it was, the document explained, his warped interest in eyes that had led him to kill.

It ended with a warning in capitals:

KAINE IS NOT TO BE APREHENDED
WITHOUT LEVEL 3 BACKUP

Sixty-nine

CEM KEMAL HAD worked at the CIA's Istanbul Bureau for four and a half years and was a rising star in the agency. Hailing from a prominent Turkish family, he had been born and raised in the United States and was regarded as a natural bridge between East and West.

Perusing the briefing on Kaine that morning, Kemal hadn't had much of a reason to be interested. The idea of psycho surgeons devouring human eyes seemed a world away — the kind of thing you would find in Indiana, not Istanbul. As for oculosis, which the brief explained Kaine had been trying to cure, Agent Kemal knew very little about that either. The disease had affected Greece and Bulgaria badly, and was only now making its way eastward through Turkey.

Pulling his suede jacket from the coat stand behind the door, Kemal went down to the garden of the Çorlulu Ali Paşa Medresesi.

Located across the street from his office, the garden was a veritable sanctuary where he was a regular, enjoying nothing more than whiling away the hours in its shade. Taking coffee there was both a glorious ritual — one that spanned late afternoon and early evening — and an education in modern Turkey.

The waiter glided over, tray in hand. Placing a glass of thick coffee on the chipped vinyl tabletop, he ambled away. Everyone who came in drank the same bitter coffee, sweetening it to taste with a miniature mound of sugar-lumps.

A moment later the waiter returned with a shisha water-pipe. He fired it up with hot coals and a little apple tobacco, before presenting Kemal with the end of the pipe.

Over the next hour or so, a stream of informers drifted in and out, revealing fragments of information. None were of any special interest. None, that is, except for Mustafa the shoemaker's son. He delivered a page ripped out from a child's exercise book, which consisted of three sentences. They described how a doctor from Belarus was helping at a small private hospital, Clinic Samsun. On the face of it, the information was uninteresting, but a detail caught Agent Kemal's eye.

At the end of the handwritten note were the words:

Boy aged 10 cured of oculosis.

Waving a hand to the waiter, Kemal paid the bill and walked the short distance down to Sultanahmet. Within a few minutes he was striding through the doorway of Clinic Samsun.

Seventy

Twisting his body upright, Kaine put his feet on the floor and took a long, determined breath. As a surgeon, he knew that the worst thing to do was to panic. And so, coaxing himself to remain calm, he made an examination of each eye using his fingertips.

The area just below each one was sore and hard, and the eyeball itself felt as though it had been baked in a hot oven for a very long time. But most alarming was the way that the optic nerve was sending a stream of vivid colours to his brain, scrambling all other thoughts.

Even though Kaine had not lived in the Bebek villa long, he had an obsessive attention to detail — one that helped him map out the geography of the house in his mind. Replaying every inch, he pictured the pieces of furniture and the artwork, the doorframes, the windows, and the precise length and breadth of each room. The key was going to be visualizing the exact layout of the makeshift laboratory.

Feeling his way downstairs, the surgeon went through to it.

In the far right corner stood a small refrigerator, one of the old ones from just after the war. He opened it, delved inside, and pulled out his hand. In its claw-like grip were the last three eyes.

Kaine swallowed them in one gulp. He didn't even chew.

If he was to sort himself out, he knew that he needed the biggest intellectual rush of his life.

The eyes having been chilled for many days, it took them a few minutes to be broken down. Slowly, the surgeon sensed their amino acids entering his bloodstream and finding their way into his brain.

All of a sudden, his mind lit up.

Channelling the myriad of thoughts, Kaine watched himself as if from a great height, as though looking down at his situation, observing it as an outsider. With great care, he regarded the extraordinary array of apparatus laid out before him, the vials of chemicals, the microscope and the centrifuge, the imaging devices, the gauges and the diagnostic gear.

Without eyesight, most of it was completely useless. He began to hyperventilate and then to shake. Something inside his head was telling him to give himself up.

But, again calming himself, Kaine moved over to the work table. He dug the base of each hand into his eye sockets.

Then he thought like he had never thought before.

He thought of every person he had examined who suffered from oculosis and how the various stages of the disease were manifested. He thought, too, of the way the virus had made the leap from poultry to man, and how it had mutated so quickly. After that, he cross-referenced everything he had seen and heard about the virus with his encyclopaedic knowledge of the nervous system and the human eye.

For an hour or more he sat there, processing millions and millions of separate thoughts.

And, slowly, a pattern revealed itself.

It wasn't another breakthrough, but it was a pattern nonetheless.

Fumbling in the drawer of the desk opposite the door, Kaine removed three glass vials. Two of them contained an antiviral drug he had been working on. The third was filled with chicken blood. Breaking open the vials one by one, he did his best to conduct a series of final experiments on them. But being blind as he now was, it was almost impossible to examine the results.

At the end of the experimentation, the doctor cursed and hurled the vials at the wall. He thought of giving up, of mixing a suicidal cocktail and downing it in one. Suicide was the loser's way out, though, and Amadeus Kaine was damned if he was going to quit the world a loser.

Flexing his back muscles, he braced himself. He was a survivor, and what survivors did best was to succeed when the odds were hopelessly stacked against them.

He picked out three more vials and ran another series of tests, then another, and another, and then fifty more.

For five days and nights he laboured away, uncertain of the hour or indeed of whether it was day or night. The only indication of the passing of time was the muezzin calling the faithful to prayer five times through each day. He didn't eat, or sleep, but felt more exhilarated than any man alive.

Then, suddenly, he stopped.

Before him was a glass test tube containing a wheat-coloured liquid. Holding the end of the tube to his nostrils, he took a long, considered whiff. It had a scent of roasted walnuts.

Kaine took a syringe from the cupboard, fumbled to remove the packaging and to attach a needle. Then, with extreme care, he withdrew thirty millilitres of the liquid and, without any ceremony, injected it into his leg.

Ten seconds later, he was lying unconscious on the floor.

Seventy-one

ALMOST A THOUSAND delegates were packed into the Sails Pavilion at the San Diego Conference Center, each one there by special invitation. The three-day event had drawn leading professionals from the world of bio-tech, all of them united by a single goal — to find a cure for oculosis. And, more importantly, to make a fortune having done so.

At the podium, the keynote speaker, Professor Michael Doffman, was concluding a lecture on the recent work in achieving an antiviral response to oculosis.

'And so, as I said, my fellow colleagues, I do believe that we have the ability to find a solution to this catastrophic scourge of nature. I urge us all to forget our differences and to come together at this challenging time. After all, oculosis can't be beaten by one man alone. Its pathology is, as you are all aware, extraordinarily complex. But there is a glimmer of hope. Our research teams have confidence that the disease will have at least a rudimentary cure within three to five years.'

Applauded for his speech, Professor Doffman took questions when it was over. A man in the front row stood up, snatched the microphone, and asked:

'Professor, I know that everyone seated here has the same name on all their tongues, a name that you did not mention in your lecture — Dr. Amadeus Kaine. Where is Kaine and why isn't he helping his country?'

Professor Doffman listened to the question, and to the murmur that moved gradually through the conference pavilion in its wake.

'As an ophthalmologist myself,' he said, 'I can tell you unequivocally that Dr. Kaine has brought nothing but shame on the field. He has single-handedly set back the business of finding a cure by many months, and even years. I counsel you all to shun Kaine and his contributions. The man is a liability, a charlatan and, I hope, he's nothing more than a dead star. Why don't we all try to forget that he ever existed?'

Seventy-two

AT THE SAME moment that Professor Doffman was answering questions in San Diego, a Cray XK6 mainframe was crunching data concerning viral oculosis at CIA headquarters. Since the sudden disappearance of Amadeus Kaine, the Agency had contacted every bureau and every informant in an effort to locate the rogue surgeon.

There had been sightings on five continents — including in a shopping mall in Yokohama and at a public swimming pool outside Adelaide, on the fiftieth floor of the Empire State Building, and on a cruise ship bound for the Seychelles.

The dossier of Kaine's international client base was pored over by a special team of agents. They examined every journey he had made to treat an endless catalogue of dictators, oligarchs, and VIPs the world over.

The CIA and the FBI had been watching Kaine for years. Both agencies had approached him time and again, cajoling him to work on their behalf. But, having been raised with a firm contempt for the bureaucracy of government, the eye surgeon had rejected all offers. He had instead cut out the middlemen and, as a result, had achieved unprecedented access to a *Who's Who* of world leaders.

At 3.22 a.m. on the morning after the San Diego Bio-tech Conference began, the Cray XK6 sent a closed system email to its controller. It read, simply:

CIA Istanbul Bureau. Code FIT08/43. Believe Kaine to be using alias Victor Oskovich. Operating from Clinic Samsun. Agent Kemal making investigation.

Seventy-three

As THE SUN rose above the Bosphorus, its rays glinting across the surface of the great waterway, the thumb on Kaine's right hand twitched once, then again.

A minute of stillness passed, and the fingers trembled very slightly. Then another pause and the surgeon's head jolted to the side. Within an hour, he was sitting upright, having pulled himself into the corner of the room.

A shaft of bright winter sunlight had broken through a hole in the shutters and was reflecting off a patch of floor like a natural laser beam. Crumpled up in the corner, Kaine stared at it, too fearful to move lest it disappear.

For an hour he watched the light as its angle increased.

He couldn't believe it. Even as a blind man he had managed to create the golden formula to restore sight. Yes, it needed some refinement, but that was quite achievable with careful measurement — the kind that was near impossible without the power of sight.

Slowly, Amadeus Kaine got to his feet and examined his eyes in a hand mirror. The swelling and the hardness had vanished, and his eyes were the same bottle-green hue as they had always been. Overcome with euphoria, the surgeon put his hands to his eyes once again.

And this time he wept.

For three more days he worked on fine-tuning his formula. The beauty of it was the stark simplicity. Comprising seven chemicals, all of them easily procured, Kaine's cure for oculosis was one that challenged the disease at cell level. He named it K-7.

Exhausted and weak, he mixed up four litres of it, put on his clothes, and took a cab down to Clinic Samsun.

Within an hour, the antiviral drug was being injected into patients. Briefing the staff, Kaine explained that K-7 was to be administered on an empty stomach, and in one universal dose of twenty millilitres. The patients were to lie in darkness for up to a day after treatment, and were only then to be exposed gradually to light. Such was the sense of desperation that no one questioned what was in the drug, or whether it had been licensed.

All morning Kaine administered the antivirus, giving it to more than a hundred victims. Having taken their dose, they lay out in the clinic's corridors and its cramped wards, as Samsun's director paced up and down fretfully.

'This is the moment when we pray, Dr. Oskovich,' he said.

'There's nothing wrong with prayer,' Kaine replied. 'It can make all the difference.'

The director stopped pacing. He wiped a hand over his bald head.

'I forgot to tell you,' he mumbled, 'that your friend was here.'

'My friend? Which friend?'

'A Turkish man with an American accent.'

'When did he come?'

'Oh, several times. Two or three days ago, and then again last night.'

Kaine was so drained he couldn't think straight. He was craving the delicious texture of a nice green eye. The thought of it made him salivate. Just then a pretty nurse from the Mediterranean coast walked by. She had wonderfully virescent eyes, and smiled as she passed. Something deep in his gut was telling Kaine to follow her, to ask her out, and then to enjoy her with a glass of the local raki.

But he was a reformed character now.

Complimenting himself on his sense of altruism, he was amused at robbing the drug companies of their profits. There wasn't a pharmaceutical giant on the planet that wouldn't have paid millions — or even billions — for K-7.

And there he was, giving it away for free.

He had to get the formula up on the internet, so that it was in the hands of the people and not the pharmaceutical firms.

Suddenly, he remembered what the director had said, that his supposed friend was looking for him. For all he knew it was a bio-tech company that had tracked him down. After all, they were well known to out-spy governments.

Walking through to Dr. Evren's office, Kaine logged online and began uploading the formula to a bio-tech noticeboard. He had half of it up, when there was a knock at the door.

'Dr. Oskovich,' said a nurse. 'Your friend, he's come.'

'My friend?'

'Yes, the one who came before.'

Kaine froze. Then, peeking through the crack in the door, he got a good look at Agent Kemal. Everything about him said CIA — from the rubber-soled loafers to the small spiral notebook in his shirt pocket.

He thought of bluffing his way through. Experience had shown him that the CIA was nothing but a circus full of clowns.

Reaching for the handle, he began to pull the door open. He had a valid Belarus passport, and the clinic's staff would have vouched for him. But if the agent had spent any time in the US, he would have guessed at once that he was no Victor Oskovich from deepest darkest Belarus.

No. No. Bluffing it would be suicide.

Kaine pushed the door closed. Quickly, he opened the window and jumped through onto the grass.

Five minutes after that he was in the alleyway outside the eye bank. Like a moth to a flame, he couldn't help himself. He needed an eye — or rather a handful — in order to think.

The best thing about eye banks is that they're not regarded as terrorist targets, or the kind of places from which valuable medical equipment can be stolen. So, their security is never very strong — even in the time of oculosis.

Scoping the building out, Kaine noticed that there was a little open window on the ground floor. It looked like a supply cupboard, located beside a much larger room, the one Kaine supposed housed the refrigeration units.

He waited until sunset, when the staff began leaving for the night. A security guard was standing near the main door, smoking a cigarette and talking to his girlfriend on a mobile phone. He was young, no more than twenty, his mind clearly a thousand miles away.

Summoning all his strength, Kaine crouched low and ran over the parking area, on the other side of the building from the main door. He moved along the brick wall, up to the open window.

Thirty seconds later he was inside.

A minute after that, he had located the refrigeration units and was decanting the eye bank's stock into a daypack he had bought that afternoon. The only problem was that, in the rush, there was no way of telling which eyes were green. Growling to himself, Kaine took anything he could get, zipped up the bag, and made his escape.

Outside, the security guard was lighting a second cigarette. Laughing, he blew kisses into the phone. The American doctor walked right past him, the daypack slung casually over his right shoulder.

Suddenly, he heard the muffled sound of feet moving fast across tarmac. Even before turning, he recognized it — the rubber-soled loafers.

Kaine bolted.

He rushed down the alley that curled around the back of the eye bank. Then, turning sharp right, he made his way past a row of cheap hotels and out by the German Fountain, in the direction of the Hagia Sophia.

Behind him, moving at lightning speed, the rubber soles were catching up. The CIA man wasn't weighted down by a daypack full of human eyes. He had the added advantage of knowing the area, too.

The great mosque loomed up into the early evening sky; Kaine hurried towards it. He could see tourists heading in the opposite direction, the building having closed up for the day. Skirting around to the right, he passed the ablutions fountain and the wall of the baptistery. A moment later, he was hiding in a niche between two doors. It was so small that he had to squeeze in sideways.

There was a sense of safety there but, even better, there were steps leading down.

The doctor descended, and found himself in an underground passageway illuminated by a series of low-watt bulbs. It zigzagged northwards for half a mile or so. Running to the end, Kaine reached another staircase. Resting for a moment against the damp, graffiti-covered wall, he opened the daypack and scoffed a handful of the eyes.

They may have been cold but in the circumstances they tasted divine.

Amadeus Kaine stood on the bottom step, too exhausted to run up into the outside world. For some strange reason he wasn't pumped full of energy from the eyes. Instead, he crouched down and fell into a deep, childlike sleep.

All of a sudden he was eleven years old, tracking through the forest with his young cousin, Pete. It was high summer and the trees were emerald green, the blistering afternoon air abundant with butterflies and hope.

A Davy Crockett hat pulled down tight on his head and a pair of Algonquian moccasins on his feet, Amadeus was leading the way back to the camp when he spotted something.

Partly concealed in bracken, it was large, brown, and camouflaged against the undergrowth. Making their way over to it gingerly, the boys found a great male buck. Its body was still warm, as though it had died moments before from a heaving wound to its underside.

It was the first time that Amadeus had been with a creature so soon after death. He bent down and pressed his face to the shank. It smelled pungent and proud, as if connected to nature in the most basic way.

Fumbling for his pocket-knife, Amadeus opened up the longest blade. Then, as if something inside him was telling him what to do, he cut out the buck's eyes one at a time. His hands bloodied, he packed up the eyes in birch leaves and took them back to his uncle's cabin.

That night, locked away in his room, he examined them with a torch and a magnifying glass. From that day on, all he could think about was the organ that shapes our world by giving us sight.

Seventy-four

THE MORNING AFTER the anti-viral injections had been administered at Clinic Samsun, there was a resounding sense of alarm. Men, women and children were screaming, weeping, and jumping up and down — with joy.

They could see.

By lunchtime, hundreds more sufferers of oculosis were arriving from across the Turkish capital. All were informed that the antiviral drug had run out, and that its creator — the elusive Belarusian surgeon Dr. Oskovich — had vanished as mysteriously as he had come.

The Turkish media besieged the clinic, demanding to know how the dreaded oculosis could have been reversed. Within an hour or two, satellite trucks from every major news channel were parked outside the building. Inside, an army of international reporters hounded the Anatolian director for answers.

Agent Kemal had spent much of the night crisscrossing Sultanahmet, asking his informers what they had seen. But the trail had gone dead, and the incomparable Amadeus Kaine had escaped.

Again.

Seventy-five

HAVING SPENT THE night at the end of the tunnel, the American eye surgeon emerged an hour before dawn. He knew all that mattered was getting to a computer to upload the formula. The grave danger would be a single bio-tech firm getting hold of it. In his less-than-credible position, Kaine knew he would have to tread with great care.

He crossed the street and made his way to a 24-hour internet café, the kind patronized by girls trying to hook a boy six time zones to the west. There was no one in there except for a wiry young man at the desk. He scribbled out a slip of paper with a time.

'Number six,' he said.

Kaine went over to the computer and logged on. It took a few minutes to access the bio-tech noticeboard. Once he was there, he began typing in the formula and the breakdown of instructions. He got further than before, and detailed the complex third stage of the process.

As he read it through, he heard a man's voice behind him. Assuming it was just another customer, he didn't bother to turn.

'You're under arrest,' said the man, in an American accent.

Kaine looked up.

Then, quickly, he reached for the mouse, dragging the cursor to the SEND button. But before he could click, his right hand was jerked away, forced behind his back, and cuffed.

Agent Kemal barked an instruction in Turkish.

A pair of police officers marched in. Before he could protest, Kaine was dragged out and thrown into the back of an armoured police van.

Seventy-six

AT THE FBI headquarters, Special Agent Marris punched the air when he heard the news. He may not have caught the eye surgeon himself, but he felt as though he had been instrumental all the same. Online, he found a copy of the extradition treaty between the United States and Turkey, which had been signed more than thirty years before. There was always wrangling over the details, but Marris knew that the last thing Turkey would want was to have a cannibalistic American in its jails.

After lunch, he picked up the phone and called his contact in the US Extradition Service.

'Hey Frank, it's Harry Marris up in New York. Got a quick one for you. What's the usual in extraditions between Turkey and the US?'

Agent Marris took a sip from the polystyrene cup on his desk. He grimaced.

'That long? Yeah. That's right. Yeah, it's him — Cannibal Kaine.'

That evening, just as Marris was about to leave, he got a call on the secure line. It was FBI headquarters down in DC.

'Marris here.'

A voice came on the line, a voice Agent Marris recognized at once as that of the Agency's director, Thomas W. Griff.

'Hello, sir.'

'Marris, as you know, we're bringing Kaine back Stateside. But we're cutting through the red tape. A situation has arisen.'

'A situation, sir?'

'It's classified. But it's gonna move the wheels a whole lot faster than normal.'

'Faster, sir?'

'That's right. We're looking to get Kaine back here by the end of next week.'

'Excellent, sir.'

'Marris?'

'Yes, sir?'

'This matter is highly sensitive. We're working in association with the CIA and Turkey's NIO. Pack your bags pronto. You're going to Istanbul.'

Seventy-seven

ANXIOUS THAT HE might be knifed if put in with the general prison population, or even in solitary, the Turkish authorities had taken the unusual step of incarcerating their American prisoner in a military jail to the west of Istanbul. A vile, stinking hellhole, it was the kind of institution where enemies of the state were generally locked up and forgotten.

Kaine's cell was eight feet square with a ribbed concrete floor, a central drain and a squat toilet. There was no furniture, and no window. The only source of light was a pipe no wider than a garden hose. It ran in a straight line from the cell to the exterior wall. Pressing his nose up to it, Amadeus Kaine found that he could smell the freshness of the outside world.

Unlike most of the cell's former occupants, he didn't mind being incarcerated in solitary. It gave him time to think, and to entertain himself with the definite sense of tranquillity. He slipped into the routine that forms a framework to those of an obsessive nature.

Morning, night, and through the day, he would go through the ritual of touching key points — the third screw on the left of the door, a triangular chip of paint on the wall, and the end of the air pipe. As the days passed, the rituals grew more elaborate. He would run through complex counting progressions for each key point.

For five days Kaine sat there, preoccupied by the obsessions. The more he gave in to them, the more entrenched he became, until he couldn't imagine ever re-entering normal society again.

During the nights he experienced moments of desperate craving for human eyes, and agonizing headaches from withdrawal. He cursed himself for not feasting on all the eyes from the Sultanahmet eye bank when he had the chance. But most of all, he cursed Agent Kemal for cuffing him seconds before he had made the formula for K-7 public.

The formula. It was the one way to solve a crisis threatening to eliminate millennia of human history. Looking at the virus from the distance of the cell, Kaine was almost amused. He could see the progression clearly. Oculosis would continue to mutate exponentially and would soon have infected the majority of the world's population. Without the K-7 antivirus, the endgame was assured — every man, woman and child on the planet would go blind.

And then, within days or weeks, human society would disintegrate, as new predators rose up and conquered them. It was just a question of which species would come first — rats, cockroaches, or the insects that live in the shadow of man.

Kaine considered how, in centuries past, such radical and rapid infection would have been unthinkable. The Black Death and the influenza pandemics might have been devastating, but neither was in the same league as oculosis.

And it was all due to the factory farming of chickens. Who would have thought such a seemingly sensible idea to provide cheap food could have led to this? The virus's pathology, mixed with the flow of human movement, had led to an exponential diffusion. The human race had signed its own death warrant by cutting costs and streamlining on an industrial scale.

Kaine took a long, hard breath of fresh air from the hosepipe.

How could he get the formula for K-7 into the open? Having mastered thirteen languages while so invincible in the early days of eating human eyes, he translated the formulaic code into each one in his head.

Given a chance, he would have written the formula down. He had found a soft-tipped pen in a niche up high in his cell, hidden there by a former inmate.

Kaine cursed his luck. There wasn't any paper. But, even if there had been, there was no point in writing the formula down if there was no way to get it out into the open.

On the sixth day of solitary confinement, he heard the sound of shoes walking slowly over stone. They weren't the sturdy leather soles of the guards' boots, but rather they were softer, a lighter grade of leather.

The rubber soles of American loafers.

Kaine sat up.

There was the dull clunk of a steel key being inserted into the door lock, metal pressing on metal, and a bolt retracting into the mechanism.

The next thing the surgeon knew, Special Agent Marris was standing over him.

'You're going home, Cannibal Kaine.'

'How nice.'

'I doubt it will be,' said Marris.

Seventy-eight

AN ELABORATE ROUTINE followed.

It involved harnesses and straitjackets, blindfolds, face guards and tempered steel manacles. Having begun in the Turkish solitary confinement cell, it ended in a secret military base north of New York.

It was a bitterly cold day, the concrete ground outside a skating rink of frost. On landing, Special Agent Marris called his wife, to be told that their son, Harry Jr., had started having seizures. They were driving in a blacked-out vehicle from the airstrip to an undisclosed FBI location in New England.

Kaine had overheard the conversation.

'It's the next phase in the pathology,' he said softly. 'I'm assuming your son has gone blind in both eyes.'

Marris looked round at the surgeon, whose face was enveloped in a canvas hood, his mouth covered with a muzzle beneath.

'How dare you listen in!'

'Is it both eyes?' Kaine repeated.

Marris sighed.

'*Yes.*'

'You know there's a cure... A cure for oculosis.'

'Next thing you'll be telling me that you came up with it.'

'I did.'

'So where is it?'

'It's in my head.'

After the fifty-minute drive through a bleak landscape peppered with naked pines and juniper trees, the vehicle drew to a halt at what looked like a military fortress. There were electrified fences and watchtowers, razor wire, guards, and the usual sense of understatement, as if enormous firepower was concealed inside.

Amadeus Kaine was searched three times over, then given a medical examination. Following that, he was taken to a clean, new interrogation room. The far wall had a panel of one-way bulletproof glass in the middle. The only furniture was a cheap government-issue table and a pair of matching chairs.

Kaine had done enough work with governments to know the scent of the secret service. He waited for Agent Marris to come back in, and for the threats to start. But, to his surprise, another agent entered. He was older than Marris, obviously more senior, with more expensive shoes and a better cut of suit. He motioned to an officer standing guard at the door.

A moment later, Kaine's wrists were free.

'Things are looking up,' he said.

The newcomer sat down. He looked at Kaine hard, as though sizing him up before getting down to business. The eye surgeon just sat there, staring into space. In his mind he was counting the painted breeze blocks that made up the wall.

'My name is Thomas Griff,' said the man in the suit. 'I'm the Director of the FBI.'

Kaine emitted a piercing laugh.

'I'm getting VIP treatment, am I?' he said.

Griff rested his hands on the vinyl tabletop and leaned forward.

'I'm not here because I want to be,' he replied. 'The Agency has a file on you as thick as the NYNEX directory. We know you're pally with every failed state this side of Mogadishu, but...'

'But,' said Kaine, breaking in, 'it seems there's a reason that's driven you to rush through the hoops of the extradition process. I can't imagine that was easy.' He paused, smiled through the corner of his mouth. 'I wonder what it is,' he said.

'Oculosis.'

'Ah, fancy that.'

'We understand that you have been working on an antiviral drug.'

'Do you, now?'

'Yes.'

'Well maybe I have, and maybe I haven't.'

'How close are you to completing it?'

Kaine shrugged.

'You know how long these drugs take to bring to market,' he said. 'Years... decades even.'

Director Griff touched a thumbnail to his paisley tie.

'We can speed things up,' he said.

'I'm sure you can,' said the surgeon. 'And I'm guessing you'd make billions and billions for yourselves in doing so. After all, I'm assuming you would plan to patent the formula and produce it yourselves.'

The director stood up. He walked over to the mirror and made a signal. A moment later, another agent came in. In his hand was a slim dossier, marked TOTAL SECRECY.

Passing it to the director, he went out.

'I want you to look at this sheet of paper and to give me your analysis,' said Griff.

'What is it?'

'A medical report.'

The director placed the sheet on the table. It was filled with ten-point text, with the words TOP SECRET stamped in each corner in red.

Focusing hard, Kaine looked at it for fifteen seconds.

'What do you want to hear from me?' he asked.

'Your opinion.'

'The patient has what I would call omnigenous-oculosis. That means that he has contracted a mutated form of the virus, one that will almost certainly lead next to seizures. You can ask Agent Marris about it, if you like.'

'Will the antiviral drug — your antiviral drug — work against it?'

Amadeus Kaine wagged a finger in the direction of the FBI chief.

'You're putting words in my mouth,' he said. 'I never said that I had developed an antivirus.'

Griff held out a hand.

'OK, let's imagine that you had developed an antivirus. Would it be effective in this case?'

'Possibly. But only with surgical intervention.'

'Who in the United States has the skill to perform such an operation?'

The surgeon glanced down at the floor. He seemed to blush.

'Only me,' he said.

Seventy-nine

AT 5.20 NEXT morning, Amadeus Kaine was moved by military helicopter to Fort Meade, Maryland. He was blindfolded and chained for the flight. At the army base, he was transferred to solitary confinement. He waited there for three days, while the FBI, the military, and the government's most senior staff argued.

With their backs up against the wall, the question was whether the eye surgeon could be trusted. No one believed he could. He was after all a cannibal, and the most depraved kind at that.

The subject was so sensitive that only the eleven men and women of the Emergency Operation Unit were briefed. The security threat level was so high that almost no details were actually vocalized. Any names spoken were concealed by code words. The patient was known simply as 'Mr. Jones'.

After endless hours of often heated debate, a tall, grey-suited man gestured for silence. Older than the others, he had an air of distinction, and an expression of severe clinical coldness.

'From where I am sitting,' he said in a stern, rasping voice, 'there's nothing left to discuss. Left untreated for another day or two, Mr. Jones will be dead.'

Director Griff slammed the table with his fist.

'Are you telling me that you're gonna let a cannibal do it?'

'There's no one else who even comes close,' said the man in grey. 'I want to take a vote, right now. If you agree that we use Kaine, put up your hand.'

Five hands were raised instantly. Then, angrily, Griff raised his, too.

Eighty

IT TOOK A full day for the vote to pass through all necessary government channels. When it had finally been signed off, Griff travelled from FBI headquarters in Washington to Fort Meade. He wanted to handle the negotiation with Kaine himself.

The prisoner was doing push-ups in his cell when the director arrived. He looked leaner than at the previous meeting, as though the lack of eyes had somehow robbed him of some fat. Although weakened by a break from the illicit diet, he had learned to conjure a reserve of primeval strength that lies deep within us all.

Ten minutes after Griff's arrival, Kaine was cuffed and manacled, then transferred to a holding cell at the end of the solitary block. There were a pair of chairs in there, a low table, and a large patch of dried blood on the floor.

The director took off his wristwatch, a vintage Rolex, and placed it on the table.

'I'm going to make you an offer,' he said. 'Then I will give you a full minute to think before you give me a reply.'

'Sounds intriguing,' said Kaine.

'The case study I showed you the other day,' Griff said, his voice trembling, 'is that of a VIP who needs urgent treatment.'

'Judging by what you showed me, his time's running out,' the doctor replied. 'What's ya offer?' he asked in a faux-Cockney voice.

'I'll keep you away from the chair if you perform the operation.'

'Oooh, lovely, a life rotting in solitude. I think I'd rather fry.'

The director wiped a hand over his face and breathed in.

Amadeus Kaine could see his pupils were dilated, suggesting extreme anxiety.

'Your vision's blurring, is it?' he said.

Director Griff stood up. He placed his chair right next to the surgeon's and sat down again. They were inches from each other.

'Do the operation perfectly and then we'll talk.'

Kaine rolled his eyes.

'I'm not even going to dignify that offer with an answer,' he said. 'C'mon, make me a real offer. I can hear your nice old watch ticking.'

'Thirty years,' said Griff. 'I'll get you thirty years and after that you walk.'

'I'll be dead in half that from boredom!'

'Twenty!'

'*Pah!*'

Kaine leaned an inch closer to the FBI director. He could smell the adrenalin in his sweat. It stank like cat piss.

'I think we're doing this the wrong way round,' he said. 'So I'm going to make *you* an offer. But unlike the offers you're giving me, mine isn't negotiable. It's take it or leave it.'

Amadeus Kaine leaned back and flexed his right shoulder. 'As you've noticed,' he said, 'you need me a whole lot more than I need you. And for that reason I'd say that I'm in what they call a privileged position.'

The director was about to interject, but Kaine cocked his head towards the Rolex.

'I'll treat your patient with my formula, and will then operate on him. He'll be good as new, and in return you set me free.'

Griff slapped his hands together.

'No frigging way! You're a cannibal, a frigging cannibal, and a psycho one at that!'

Amadeus Kaine grinned meekly.

'And I'm the only man alive who can save your friend,' he said.

Eighty-one

THAT EVENING, THE eye surgeon was sitting cross-legged in his cell, rocking gently back and forth. Lost in the labyrinth of his mind, he was counting the brushstrokes in a painting from Picasso's Blue Period. His attention drifting, he closed his eyes for a moment and saw Francine there.

She was pitched against a backdrop of darkness and her hair was tied up tight on the back of her head. As he watched her, she smiled. But it wasn't a smile from when they had first met. Rather, it was a cold smile inspired by vengeance, from the torturous days of her affairs.

Trembling, her lips melted into a scowl. Beckoning him to follow, she led him through into a cavernous baroque hall. Although conjured from his imagination, it was decorated from a knowledge of his ex-wife's mind.

The floor was adorned with Persian tapestries and was illuminated by giant candelabra.

The walls were hung with dismembered heads.

One by one, Amadeus Kaine took them in. They were the heads of his colleagues and his friends, his relatives and of distant acquaintances. All of them had their throats slashed.

'What have you done?' he asked her in horror.

Francine touched a hand to her cheek impishly.

'I have killed them for you,' she replied.

'How?'

'With shame.'

Only later did the surgeon comprehend Francine's grand plan. For weeks she had engaged in a series of affairs with her husband's closest colleagues and friends. Then, one morning, she revealed the most intimate and sordid details of her double life to the tabloid press.

A laughing stock, Kaine was lampooned by almost everyone who knew him, and by plenty of others who were following the twists and turns of it all in the press.

It had taken the surgeon years to restore his reputation.

Finally, divorced and back at the top of his profession, he vowed solemnly never again to allow anyone to get close to him. As far as he was concerned, his private life was locked down. Devoting himself to a regime of secrecy, Kaine carried on and rose to new heights. And all the while he tried to forget the name Francine.

There was the jingle of keys and the guard unlocked the door.

'They want you,' he said, cuffing the prisoner's wrists behind his back.

'Who do?'

'The big guns.'

After numerous twists and turns, Kaine was brought to an interrogation room one level above his cell. All that day he had been craving a succulent green eye, and had imagined it served up with a trace of truffle oil and a sprinkle of grated wasabi.

Director Griff was sitting at the other end of the room, along with an elderly man in a handmade grey suit.

The FBI director waited for Kaine to be uncuffed. When he was seated on the other side of the table, he jerked a thumb towards the man in grey.

'This is Mr. Zanawski.'

The prisoner blinked a greeting.

'Hello,' he said.

Griff glanced at his Rolex. This time he didn't take it off. He appeared even more anxious than he had before.

'The seizures have started,' he said.

'When?'

'Three hours ago.'

'Then I'd say that your time's running out,' said Kaine.

Zanawski strained to smile. He didn't know the surgeon, but didn't like him if first impressions and a thick case file were anything to go by.

'If Mr. Jones makes a full recovery, you'll be released,' he said sternly.

'*Mr. Jones?*'

The man in grey wove his fingers together.

'The President of the United States,' he said.

Eighty-two

To PREPARE THE antiviral drug and then to perform the operation, Kaine required a cutting-edge ophthalmological unit. He refused point blank to have anything to do with military installations, or to work at a makeshift lab or operating theatre. The risks of either, he said, were far too great, and he couldn't risk being stuck with the blame. Only the best of the best would, he insisted, guarantee success.

After far too much debate, the Emergency Medical Crisis Unit agreed to bring Kaine to the George Washington University Hospital, a block north of the Foggy Bottom subway stop in the heart of the capital.

Special Agent Marris had flown down from New York, and was in charge of the prisoner. Seated in the back of a convict transport vehicle together, they made light conversation. Ahead of them, and behind them, there were four army Humvees, with police snipers on surrounding rooftops and an air support helicopter cruising the sky.

Dressed in a pair of prison-issue trousers, with a white T-shirt and a leather jacket he had bought in Istanbul before his arrest, Dr. Kaine didn't look much out of the ordinary, except that his wrists were cuffed together and he was wearing military-issue manacles.

As they approached the hospital, Marris seemed anxious. He listened to the crackle of a voice on the short-wave radio, then signalled through to the driver. The vehicle slowed and the back door opened, deluging the cell with light.

His head hung low, Amadeus Kaine stepped down to the kerb, Marris leading him firmly by the arm. They took three strides.

Suddenly, a photographer rushed up.

As he did so, Kaine pulled open his jacket, threw his cuffed wrists above his head, and thrust out his chest.

Clinging tight to his torso, his white T-shirt was covered in dense, handwritten script. There were symbols, numbers, and a great block of indistinct Hindi text.

In less than three seconds the photographer had taken a dozen shots. Turning on his heel, he charged towards the subway.

'Shall I go after him, sir?' shouted one of the guards quickly.

Marris swept a hand through the air dismissively.

'We've got no time,' he said.

Leading Kaine across to the hospital entrance, they took a service elevator up to the ophthalmological department. The entire place had been locked down, with all staff and patients having been transferred. The only people there were armed soldiers and FBI agents. There were dozens of them. They were in the stairwells and the corridors, on the roofs and spread out all around the block.

With an armed guard walking in front and another behind, Marris and Kaine made their way to the sixth floor.

Turning right at the end of a long corridor, they covered the short distance to an expansive laboratory. At least twenty armed soldiers were deployed through the room in case the eye surgeon attempted to escape.

Agent Marris picked a sheet of paper from the counter.

'It's kitted out with everything you asked for,' he said.

Kaine swept an eye around the lab.

'How long do I have until Mr. Jones gets here?'

Marris looked up at the wall clock.

'An hour and a half.'

'You ask miracles of me,' said Dr. Kaine.

Eighty-three

FOLLOWING ORDERS, THE photographer got the portrait of the cannibal eye surgeon online within fifteen minutes. An hour after that, it had gone viral and had been downloaded half a million times. For anyone with a medical background and an understanding of written Hindi, it guaranteed a special surprise.

While Kaine worked away on another batch of the antiviral drug, the formula was being copied by hundreds of medical students across the Indian subcontinent and beyond. Marvelling at its elegant simplicity, they followed the instructions at the bottom of the formula that read:

URGENT: TRANSLATE AND THEN PASS ON

As news spread that a cure for oculosis was available, governments everywhere did their damnedest to get control of the K-7 formula. But it was out in the open. Despite their extensive internet monitoring systems, even the FBI was foiled.

Ten minutes after Kaine had finished creating the batch of antivirus, the president was driven in an armoured ambulance to the George Washington University Hospital. The vehicle was escorted by a cortege of military Humvees and APCs, with a pair of Apache helicopters monitoring events from the air.

His seizures having grown worse during the night, the president was convulsing every fifteen minutes. Incapacitated through blindness, he had signed over his executive powers the week before, although no information had been leaked on his condition. As far as the American people were concerned, all was well at the White House.

The president was brought up on a stretcher and wheeled fast down the sixth-floor corridor. As he turned the bend into the operating zone located beside the lab, he went into seizure.

Appearing from nowhere, a team of paramedics injected the patient with fast-acting benzodiazepine. There were shouts, the sound of feet running, and the president was rushed into the anteroom, where Director Griff was waiting.

With Marris on one side and a soldier on the other, Amadeus Kaine was brought in. He was wearing a surgical gown, having already prepped the operating theatre and scrubbed up. His wrists had been untied, but he was wearing manacles and a radio transmitter.

Director Griff had just received the FBI report of how Kaine had spread the word of his formula. Fuming, he knew there would be time later for recriminations.

Right now, all that mattered was to save the president's life.

'I am ready for him,' said Kaine in a low voice.

'You dare try anything,' the FBI director warned, 'and you'll be cut down before you can—'

Kaine held up a hand, silencing the director.

'I've got no time to listen to empty threats,' he said. 'And neither does the president.'

The stretcher was wheeled through into the theatre.

Inside, it was supremely silent. Apart from the medical team, the only other person there was a presidential close protection officer. Dressed in a surgical gown, he was holding a SIG Sauer P229 service pistol.

Once the stretcher was in position, the doors were secured shut.

The president had regained consciousness and was lying on his back. As he was transferred onto the special table, Kaine stepped forwards and touched his arm.

'My, my, what nice eyes you have, Mr. Jones,' he said.

'Are you…?'

'Dr. Amadeus Kaine. A pleasure to meet you.'

'Cannibal…'

'…Kaine,' said the surgeon with an impish smile. 'I do believe that's what they're calling me. Naughty of them, isn't it?'

The president may have been staring up at the bank of surgical lamps, but he was in complete darkness.

'I understand that you have come up with an antivirus,' he said.

'Indeed, I have. But for omnigenous-oculosis we will have to work even more magic than that.'

'What are my chances?'

Kaine caressed a hand across the president's wrist.

'Let's find out, shall we?' he replied.

Eighty-four

BY THE TIME the operation was over, the K-7 antivirus was being administered to patients in Manila, Mumbai, Hyderabad, and Doha. An hour after that, it was available in more than seventy countries worldwide.

Waiving their usually strict systems of drug testing and approval, the leading industrial nations did nothing to prevent the antivirus's immediate distribution. With blindness now affecting fifty per cent of the planet's urban population, there was nothing they could do.

Three hours after the first patients had been treated, there were whoops of joy in hospitals and homes around the world.

The war against oculosis was on.

Up on the sixth floor of the George Washington University Hospital, the President of the United States was wheeled through into a recovery room. Four White House bodyguards followed him. As soon as the surgeon had left the operating theatre, Director Griff stepped forward and cuffed his wrists.

'I seem to remember something about my freedom in return for the president's sight,' said Kaine icily.

'Who said he can see?'

'Give him an hour or two and ask him for yourself.'

Griff waved a hand at Marris.

'Get him back to the cells!'

Bristling with indignation, Amadeus Kaine regarded the FBI director with a look of death.

'That's a mistake,' he said in a voice so cold that it was barely audible.

Director Griff didn't reply.

Turning his back on Kaine, he waited for Special Agent Marris to lead the prisoner by the arm out to the corridor.

With a SWAT unit standing by on high alert, the surgeon was taken to an armoured prison vehicle waiting by the kerb.

Although Kaine had suggested he be kept around until the president's sight had returned, the FBI director had ruled against it. The only place he deemed fit for Cannibal Kaine was a super-high-security cell, the deal of freedom having been nothing more than a cheap ruse to get the operation done.

Special Agent Marris's orders were to transfer the prisoner to North Branch Correctional Institution in Maryland, about an hour's drive away. Sitting up front, he punched the address into the GPS, with Kaine locked up in the cell behind.

The vehicle moved away from the hospital, turning right onto K Street NW. It was followed by the same level of security as before, both on the ground and from the air.

A few minutes after leaving the hospital, Agent Marris put his short-wave radio to his mouth and called off the air support. When he had done that, he instructed the other armoured vehicles in the convoy to move away.

'Please confirm your security clearance,' said the lead driver over the atmospheric crackle.

Marris wiped a hand hard over his face.

'Code Two-Five-Four-Seven.'

There was a pause and the lead driver came on the short-wave again.

'Understood. Secure Unit Six-Two-One moving out.'

The armoured prison van turned left towards Columbia Heights, and was suddenly alone.

Driving through a prim residential area, it pulled up at a red-brick condo on Meridian Place.

Special Agent Marris climbed down. He opened the rear of the vehicle and escorted Kaine inside to a two-bedroom apartment on the ground floor.

A boy was lying asleep on the sitting-room couch. His mother was huddled over him, gently stroking his head. Her face was numb with fatigue and fear. She looked up as her husband came in with Dr. Kaine.

'Here he is,' said Marris. 'As for the equipment you asked for, it's in the bedroom.'

'When was the last seizure?'

'Five minutes ago, but they're getting worse,' the woman said.

Kaine held out his wrists.

'If I'm gonna operate, I'll need to work freely.'

Marris undid the cuffs.

The surgeon motioned to the manacles.

'These too.'

'You're on your honour,' Marris said sternly, unlocking them.

'Don't you dare talk to me about honour!' Kaine replied. 'I've seen none of it today.'

He paused, pulled up the child's left eyelid and examined the eye.

'Show me the equipment,' he said.

They went through into the bedroom. Against the back wall was a mass of medical apparatus laid out on a long dining table. In the middle of the room there was another table and, beside it, a third one on which more specialized equipment was arranged.

Kaine looked at it all studiously. He didn't touch anything.

'This room's not sterile,' he said. 'It's not even close.'

The agent's face contorted with worry.

'Will it do?' he asked.

Amadeus Kaine didn't answer. He reached down into his groin and pulled out a vial taped to his leg.

'His condition's very unstable, the omnigenous mutation seems to affect children in an extremely virulent way. I can't promise a miracle this time,' he said. 'If you want one, I suggest you pray for it.'

The eye surgeon scrubbed up, well aware that there was hardly any point. When he was ready, he signalled to Marris, who carried the boy through.

For the next hour, Kaine toiled away at the child's eyes, fulfilling all the duties of an entire surgical team. From time to time, he heard the crackle of a short-wave out in the sitting room. From the buzz of conversation and expletives, it sounded as though the Feds assumed that their prisoner had overcome the agents and escaped.

Eighty-five

WITH EACH MOMENT that passed, the veil of oculosis was lifted a little higher, as the K-7 antivirus restored the sight of people around the world. There were celebrations in every time zone and in almost every country on Earth. A great many governments claimed to have had secretly conceived the cure, despite the fact that news of Cannibal Kaine's achievement was being widely reported.

Locked away in Agent Marris's two-bedroom condo, the surgeon finished the operation. When he was done, he paced calmly through to the sitting room.

'The boy needs time to rest,' he said.

Agent Marris was almost too fearful to pose the question on his lips.

'Do you… do you think it's been a success?' he asked.

'I told you. If you want a miracle, you'll have to pray for it.'

'We've prayed,' said Mrs. Marris, breaking down in a flood of tears. 'We've prayed and we've prayed, and we've prayed.'

The doctor's lips moved very slightly, rounding into the faintest hint of a smile.

'Then I'm hoping your prayers come true,' he said.

The short-wave crackled again. Marris glanced down at it. Then, his jaw clenching, he withdrew his service pistol.

'I'm going to give you five minutes,' he said. 'That's three hundred seconds.'

Kaine looked at the agent in disbelief.

'The operation in return for a photographer and my freedom. That's what you agreed.'

'You got the photographer. And you can have as much freedom as you can handle.'

His confusion turning to anger, Kaine scowled furiously at Marris, who cocked the trigger.

'I knew the government wouldn't keep its promise but *you* — I'd hoped that you'd be more honourable.'

Special Agent Marris raised the barrel at the surgeon's chest.

'I'm counting,' he said.

Eighty-six

CHARGING OUT OF the sitting room and through the corridor, Amadeus Kaine scooped up Mrs. Marris's purse from the hall table as he went.

A full minute later he was out on 14th Street.

A minute after that, he was in a cab heading north. The driver, an Ethiopian from Axum, thought nothing odd about picking up a customer in such a hurry, and with no clear idea of where he wanted to go.

Kaine was so overcome with rage that he needed a moment to collect his thoughts. The cab driver was in no hurry. After all, the meter was running. He started to make conversation, but the surgeon held up a hand to silence him. Looking back in the rear-view mirror, he said something in Amharic. Kaine understood and replied, his accent that of the Gondar Highlands.

'I am not having the best of days,' he said.

'I am sorry to hear that, sir,' said the driver, glancing back again.

This time Amadeus Kaine caught a look at his eyes. They were brilliant green, like a pool of phosphorescent algae.

'What marvellous eyes you have,' he said.

'Green, sir. All my family has green eyes.'

'Could you turn up here, please?'

'Left? You want to go left?'

'That's right, onto that small side street.'

'Very good, sir.'

The steering wheel shuffled anticlockwise through his hands.

'Now ease on the brake, please.'

The car came to a halt. As soon as it was motionless, Kaine reached over and snapped the driver's neck. With all his strength, he pulled the body into the back seat, then he sucked out the eyes, his tongue probing the warm ocular sockets.

'Sorry about that,' he said.

Having not feasted on the delicacy for quite some time, Dr. Kaine found the effect was immediate and rather profound.

He sensed the amino acids seeping into his bloodstream, and his brain being nourished in ways that no other food could do.

Ten minutes later, the body of the eyeless cab driver was in a dumpster, and the eye surgeon was driving himself sedately out of town. Time and again he thought about heading back to the Marris family home and availing himself of the special agent's sight.

But there would be time for that.

First things first.

Kaine needed to get set up before he got revenge. He no longer had any foreign passports or ID, but he did have access to the account at AKB Privatbank in Zurich. And there were still plenty of funds. He thought about making the call. The bank was always willing to please, and they would be only too happy to make a transfer. Any one of a dozen or more rogue states would certainly have jumped at offering him asylum.

Amadeus Kaine stroked a hand over his mouth as he drove through the northern suburbs of the capital. The world was his oyster, and only someone who has been incarcerated and chained can fully appreciate the taste of freedom.

Using the cash in Mrs. Marris' wallet, he bought himself some clothes and a few accessories. Then he killed a female jogger, feasted on her, and pondered about what to do next. He thought about visiting another eye bank, but that would have been certain suicide. Agent Marris would have anticipated it.

Marris.

He smiled at the name, and even let out a girlish giggle. Naughty little Marris would have to be punished, as would the others. Another surge of rage coursed down the surgeon's spine. It was fortified by a rush of adrenalin, one that exceeded anything he could remember. It wasn't Marris who was at fault so much as society.

The more he mused and deliberated, Kaine came to realize that the land which had produced him was to blame. The only way to make amends was to get back at all the detritus from which society was configured. He made a long hit-list in his mind of all the immoral elements — elements that would have to pay a price.

At the top of the list was the FBI.

Just below it were all the Wall Street bankers and the brain-dead celebrities. Oh, how Kaine despised the cult of celebrity. After them came the catwalk models and the politicians and the telemarketers, the sports cheats and the used-car salesmen, the tax men and the traffic wardens.

It was a simple plan, a mission in itself — one that got Kaine fired up. Reprimanding himself for pussyfooting about his entire life and for not grasping the bull by the horns, he pulled the taxi over.

He got out at a line of parked cars.

At the end of it, a Latino parking warden was writing out a ticket with a cheap ballpoint pen. Calmly, Kaine strolled up to him from behind, snapped his neck, and ate his eyes. A minute later he was back in the taxi, driving along, listening to Abba's 'Waterloo' on the radio.

He was back on track, and he was loving it.

Eighty-seven

IN THE NEXT week, Kaine crisscrossed the East Coast, causing blind terror. As people began to emerge from the darkness of oculosis, they were plunged into another nightmare — a nightmare conjured by the very man who had put an end to the previous one.

Cannibal Kaine was known to, and feared by, one and all.

Although he had used brute strength and medical know-how to break the necks of his earlier victims, he now resorted to a Colt handgun. Good fortune had provided it in the shape of an albino man in Odenton out walking his dog. In the wake of the oculosis crisis everyone, it seemed, was packing a gun.

Terrified of the thought of having their infants' eyeballs sucked out, mothers kept their children at home. Businessmen hired close-protection officers to make sure they were safe going to and from work. Celebrities doubled their security arrangements, and every law enforcement officer in the land armed themselves to the teeth.

On the first morning since operating on the president and Agent Marris's son, Cannibal Kaine killed five Chinese tourists who were shopping in downtown Baltimore. Their eyes may have been darker than he would have liked, but he found them pleasing all the same.

That afternoon, he got his mouth around a car salesman's face. Then he amused himself with his staff, turning their eyes into his lunch.

The day after that, the surgeon rose early and helped himself to a pair of security officers in Bel Air North. Laughing out loud at the ease with which he felled the great towering brutes, he bought plenty more ammunition for his little Colt, and a sound suppressor, too.

After another killing in the early evening, he moved on towards Philadelphia, and began working his way through the suburbs until he got to the city itself.

Fortunately for Agent Marris, his story had been swallowed hook, line, and sinker at the FBI. He claimed that the doctor had put a gun to his head, forcing him to call off the air support and armoured convoy. The only witness, the driver, went along with the story for a couple of hundred bucks.

By the middle of the week, eyeless bodies were being found with such frequency that widespread hysteria had turned to national panic once again. Rumour compounded the murders many times. People across the nation genuinely believed that Cannibal Kaine was at the end of their street.

Armed vigilante groups began patrolling, making spot checks on vehicles and shaking down suspicious characters. Anyone with Kaine's approximate features found themselves bloodied, beaten, or even dead.

The eye surgeon himself remained happily at large.

From Philly he travelled north-east towards New York, savouring the changing countryside. A connoisseur of human eyes, he had come to understand that the taste of his favoured fare was affected subtly by longitude.

By the time he reached Edison, Kaine had killed more than a hundred people. He felt bloated and even a little sick, but such was his craving and his enthusiasm that he couldn't stop. In his wake, he left dozens of shattered families — mothers without sons, brothers without sisters, and husbands without wives.

The striking thing about his reign of terror was that no one could work out what the motive could be. Unlike the early days, he no longer bothered to fit glass eyes, or even to use the Excisor that still bore his name. And, although his preference was for green eyes, he was willing to eat any colour now. It wasn't taste or mental stimulation that he was after, so much as good old-fashioned revenge.

As he progressed up the Eastern Seaboard, Amadeus Kaine changed vehicles often, killing the occupants and tossing the bodies out. He didn't bother to hide the corpses. They were just dead vessels as far as he was concerned.

A few miles from New York's metropolitan area, the doctor's obsessions grew alarmingly worse. So preoccupied was he at checking the rear-view mirror, that his eyes glanced back every second or two. And the counting that had plagued his whole life reached a new, acute state.

He counted the numbers of the licence plates, adding them together, and dividing by thirty-nine. He counted the vehicles moving in the opposite direction too, adding them to the licence plate tally as he went. As Manhattan approached, he counted the bumps in the road, the streetlamps, and the cars with out-of-state plates.

The journey had been a real vacation though, the kind that Kaine hadn't enjoyed in years. He couldn't believe all the fun he was having. Although there were highway patrols and police cars aplenty, none of them ever tried to pull him over — a point that confused him all the more.

Eighty-eight

THREE MILES FROM Jersey City, Amadeus Kaine thought of something — something unsettling. He had feasted on plenty of rank-and-file Americans, odious and repulsive ones at that, but hadn't so far availed himself of any celebrities. Having made a career in treating them, listening to their neuroses and pandering to their over-inflated egos, he wanted them to pay a price, too.

Pulling up at a traffic light, Kaine selected a nice dark-blue Jeep. He pretended to need directions and the vehicle's lady owner was only too pleased to help out, enticed by his phony southern drawl. A minute or two later she was dead, and her still-warm body was missing its eyes.

A short time later the surgeon was driving through the Holland Tunnel, enjoying the expectation of emerging in Manhattan.

There hadn't been a chance to throw the body of the Jeep's owner out. She was lying there, reclined in the front passenger seat. With the tunnel backed up, Kaine looked over at her.

Not bad, he thought.

An ample-busted southern belle with good thighs and thick, pouting lips, she smelled of cut-price French perfume.

Dr. Kaine looked at the empty eye sockets sitting there in a pretty face. He thought it a shame that he had not had a moment longer to spend with her while alive.

And the thought gave him another idea.

Why kill so quickly, when he might enjoy the moment of feasting all the more if his food was still alive? He cursed himself for not thinking of it before. How stupid of him. After all, almost every species except for man devours its prey live — and there was a reason.

It was fresher, and more succulent.

Eventually, the backed-up traffic began to move in fits and starts, and the Jeep emerged into the bright sunshine of a blue-sky afternoon.

The first thing Kaine did was to pull up on Canal. He wrenched the southern belle into the back. She was proving to be a distraction. He got back into the driver's seat and, as he sat there calming himself, a parking attendant sauntered over and wrote out a ticket.

Nonchalantly, the surgeon got out, opened the rear passenger door, and pushed the attendant in. Then, before killing him, he feasted on his eyes. Only then did he shoot him through the temple. After all, the last thing he wanted was an eyeless man disturbing him by making a lot of noise.

Oh, yes, he thought. Much better. Far more subtle. Even the consistency was different. Reflecting on it, he couldn't understand why President Drusnev hadn't cottoned on to the fact that human eyes were best served not only raw, but alive.

Eighty-nine

AMADEUS KAINE CLIMBED back into the driver's seat and drove slowly uptown to the Upper East Side. It was a Sunday and everyone was out, despite the headline news that Cannibal Kaine's last victim had been found across the water in New Jersey.

The reason was the weather.

New Yorkers are suckers for sunshine. There might have been a nuclear war going on, but it if was sunny, they would be out making the most of it.

Very soon, Dr. Kaine was on the Upper East Side. Words could hardly describe his elation at being back in his own stomping ground.

Every building, store and signpost sparked memories and emotions — sadness, joy, anger, sorrow, hope... and, of course, revenge.

He was so overcome that he speed-counted to a thousand in multiples of nine. And then, taking a left, he drove past his old apartment building.

Slowing to a crawl, he felt a lump in his throat.

What pain it was to be separated from the things that gave real pleasure — Wedgwood cufflinks, a favourite suit from Huntsman, or the lovely Atmos clock, which Kaine cherished above all else.

Glancing into the rear-view mirror, he remembered the parking attendant and the Jeep's owner both lying clumsily in the back. He cautioned himself to get a grip. How silly to be thinking of the past, when a splendid future was waiting to be rolled out.

His former Hollywood clients lived all over Manhattan. The island was a veritable pantry, one stocked to bursting with VIPs.

Driving through Central Park, Kaine ditched the Jeep on Museum Mile. Then he paid a visit to an old acquaintance, an elderly film director whose eyesight wasn't quite so good as it might have been. Living alone in a grand brownstone, he was a virtual recluse — one with impeccable taste. He never socialized, despite the fact that everyone in town was anxious to be seen in his company.

There was no doorman, but an entry code that hadn't changed in years. Ten minutes after Kaine's arrival downstairs, the director's eyes were digesting in the surgeon's stomach, the corpse bent over on the balcony.

Amadeus Kaine spent a little time selecting a nice suit from his host's closet. It was a little pinched at the waist, but that was the fashion after all. He showered, making use of the range of soaps from the London Ritz, and was soon reclining in the sitting room, a porcelain cup of chamomile tea nestled in his hand.

Things were going well.

Pressing his fingertips together, the surgeon wondered how they might go even better. Then another idea came to him. It was inspired, and was sure to be plenty of fun.

Having rifled through the director's address book, he picked the cream of the Hollywood crop, making marks in red against the most celebrated names. He made sure not to select anyone who had been a client of his. Then, putting on a meek and subservient voice, he called each one, pretending that he was the director's new assistant. Amazed at seeing the revered old director's name flash up on their phones, Hollywood's finest answered without hesitation.

One by one they were invited to a soirée at the director's home, one at which an important announcement was to be made.

All the next day Manhattan was abuzz with speculation about what the current Howard Hughes of Hollywood was going to say. Celebrities flaunted their verbal invitations, outshining each other. Some tweeted about it, while many who hadn't been invited pretended that they had.

At six o'clock, Dr. Kaine went into the dressing room and got ready. He put on a dark wool Italian suit with a tie from Dunhill, and a rather floral aftershave by Serge Lutens. Standing before a full-length mirror, he counted the recurring motif around the mirror's frame.

He sniffed haughtily, let out a laugh, and looked at the time on his new watch — a vintage Patek Philippe that had recently been worn on his host's bird-like wrist.

Precisely at 6.45 p.m., the guests arrived as instructed. There were twenty-three in total, each one a household name of Tinseltown royalty. Most of them knew each other, and all of them had cancelled other invitations to be present at the coup of the decade — an invitation to the legendary director's home.

The door buzzed open and the guests trooped up in the elevator, four or five at a time. Only when they were all assembled outside the apartment did Kaine open the door and introduce himself as the director's assistant. In the dim light, no one recognized him from the blurred surveillance footage on the news. In any case, the last person they expected to meet there was Cannibal Kaine.

One by one, the celebrities entered.

They did so silently, awed by the thought of actually being in such a legend's home. As they filed in, Kaine asked them politely to line up against the long wall of the grand salon. He explained that their host had planned to play out a kind of murder mystery.

Again, there was no surprise, such was the intoxicating blend of elation and emotion at having been invited. There were instead plenty of jokes, a little anxiety, and a great deal of laughter.

The surgeon disappeared for a moment or two. Then, when the guests were standing in position as instructed, he returned. Between his hands he was holding a large silver tray. Upon it were twenty-three pairs of handcuffs, and the same number of nylon cable ties.

'It's all part of the mystery,' said Kaine, rolling his eyes. 'I know it must seem odd, but he's been planning this for weeks.'

Obediently, the guests followed the instructions, tying their ankles as tight as they could, before cuffing each other's wrists.

When they were ready, Amadeus Kaine attached them one by one to an iron boom he had rigged up along the adjacent wall. By this point, the laughter was wearing thin, and the perma-tanned celebrities were eager to know what was going on.

'All will be revealed in a minute. I promise you,' said Kaine with a grin.

'You're sure you're not going to rob us!' laughed one woman, a grande dame of New York society.

'To think of it,' he replied with a smirk. 'That's the last thing I'd ever do.'

'I'm getting pretty claustrophobic here,' said a young man, known for his brazen action roles. 'I'd like to be untied. Could you grab me the key?'

Amadeus Kaine shook his head.

Then he counted to forty-two in multiples of three.

After that he turned off the lights. There were screams and exclamations, expletives, prayers, and a few tears.

And when the noise had died down, the celebrated surgeon began his work.

Ninety

THE POLICE DIDN'T arrive until well after midnight.

Plenty of people had heard the screams, but they had assumed it was a recorded scene from the director's latest movie, entitled *White Rage*. Only when the celebrities failed to come down at all did the bodyguards waiting at the kerb begin to wonder.

And wonder quickly turned to horror.

By 1.15 a.m. there were news crews from every network jostling for space at the brownstone's door. Satellite trucks were parked around the block, their technicians hustling to get their live feeds up. There were fifty police vehicles in attendance, too, and the night sky was illuminated by a pair of police helicopters. Additional arc lighting was brought in to floodlight every corner of the ground.

A SWAT team had been deployed and was combing the director's brownstone and the adjacent buildings. A dozen police snipers had taken up positions on the roofs, and the public had been evacuated from a five-block radius. A sense of raw panic ripped through Manhattan, the kind that hadn't visited the city since the morning of 9-11.

Special Agent Marris was the first FBI man at the address. Having tracked Kaine's move northwards from the capital, he knew it was just a matter of time before the doctor struck his home city.

From the doorway of the movie director's apartment he could smell the stink of fear. It was acidic on the nose, as if warning him to get out while he could. Pushing through to the sitting room, he found a young female duty officer.

'What's your report?' he said.

'Hollywood royalty, all twenty-three of them,' she said softly, her complexion ivory with fear. 'Every one was off-the-scale famous, the kind of people who are above all this.'

'Where exactly were they?'

'Here, against this wall. They were cuffed, their ankles manacled with nylon ties, trussed up to this iron rod. And their eyes...' the officer struggled to remain composed.

'He'd eaten them, hadn't he?' said Marris.

'Yes, sir. As if they were boiled candy.'

'Fatalities?'

'They were all in shock. We got them untied and out as quick as we could,' the officer said.

Marris stepped through into the bedroom. Closing the door behind him, he broke down. He couldn't stand it any more, not that he ever could.

The thought of the pain was too unbearable — having one's eyes sucked out from their sockets. Wiping his face, the agent went over to the window and looked down to the street.

It was a bright day.

He thought of all Kaine's victims, living and dead, and wondered what had gone through their minds at the moment of attack.

He chided himself for being so stupid. It didn't matter about the victims, not then. If he was going to catch the eye surgeon, he had to put himself inside Kaine's head.

Who else did he hate?

Special Agent Marris smiled.

Him.

Kaine hated him more than anyone else alive.

Ninety-one

FOR THE NEXT three days, Manhattan was shut down as if under siege.

No public transport ran and almost all the stores were closed. Most cab drivers avoided the island at all costs, and anyone who could keep away did so. All police leave was cancelled, and every street and building was combed over and over for Cannibal Kaine.

There was a sense that an unspeakable crime against every citizen had been committed, one from which the recovery would be long and excruciating. Across the nation, Americans hung black ribbons around trees in honour of their blinded actors. And, in Hollywood itself, a great many ordinary people, and celebrities, met in an unprecedented outpouring of grief.

From coast to coast, public celebrations and movie premieres were cancelled, as people reflected on why an American would be so hell-bent on attacking his own society.

Travelling up from Washington, Director Griff led the command centre at the FBI New York bureau. He was in a foul mood, having been rebuked publicly and privately by the president himself. Like everyone else in the country, he wanted to know how the cannibalistic eye surgeon had slipped so effortlessly from the Feds' incompetent grasp.

A week of public grief followed the attack on the Hollywood A-list. In that time there were plenty of sightings of Cannibal Kaine, but none that panned out. Again, the rumours and theories spread from mouth to ear, becoming more preposterous by the moment.

Kaine himself was biding his time in a bedsit near Ground Zero, having killed an elderly woman who lived in apartment 903, and feasted on her hazel eyes. He had selected the building at random, because he liked the dark green paint around the door. The curious coincidence was that his very own Mrs. Phelps lived in the building too. Her apartment,

905, was two doors down from where the doctor was lying low.

Now quite blind from oculosis, Mrs. Phelps was managing to survive by eating small cans of tuna fish in brine. She had been sent a lifetime supply the year before for dreaming up a sales line for Bill's Mexican Tuna. She had won first prize with: '*An ocean of pleasure in every can*'.

Ninety-two

IN THE DAYS since the Upper East Side attack, Amadeus Kaine did a great deal of thinking. Proud that he had made such a defiant stand against what he regarded as a rotten society, he considered how one day he would be regarded as a national hero. Indeed, in some countries — namely Iran, North Korea, Cuba, Venezuela, and Syria — he already was.

He gave thought to all the eyes he had eaten, and how everyone else alive was deluded in not consuming them as well. As far as he was concerned, ocular cannibalism was not so much about a casual delicacy as it was a way of delivering the human race to the next level of intellectual and cultural superiority.

As he sat in the little bedsit, he broke off into fits of counting every few minutes as a way of calming himself.

Suddenly, his thoughts turned to the future.

There were plenty of people out there in the world who applauded his single-handed action. He was certain that if called to arms they would join him. But there was no reason for it to be a meagre stand against an unjust world. No, no — his could be the kind of campaign that changed the very path of humanity.

Knitting his fingers together, Kaine counted them fifteen times. He thought of the summers in Cape Cod, of his childhood dog, a mongrel called Spoof, and how the first green eye to touch his lips had begun the rollercoaster ride.

Green eyes.

In all the running and the hunting, he had forgotten his love of green eyes. There was nothing else that gave the same euphoria, the same sense of supremacy.

In his brave new world, green-eyed people would be farmed.

They would be honoured of course, but raised as sacrifices for the good of the whole. There wouldn't be more green-eyed babies born naturally, as green eyes are recessive, and the gene can lie dormant for generations. And so, as Kaine pondered it, anyone giving birth to a green-eyed baby would have to hand it over and allow the state to wean it. Eventually, when called upon, green-eyed folk would proudly step forward and make the ultimate sacrifice.

In this new realm, anyone born with green eyes in the general population would be a champion, a hero of the human race. They would be fêted and saluted in the streets, regarded as preeminent sons and daughters of the master race. At the appointed age, they would be taken away and relieved of their precious asset.

The pick of the crop would be reserved for the supreme leader, while all the farmed eyes would be rationed to the proletariat. With a little time, it would lead to a vast increase in knowledge and understanding. And, eventually, the human race would abandon the confines of the forest floor… and soar up into the light.

Ninety-three

AT THE FBI command centre, Thomas W. Griff held the morning meeting as he had done each day since arriving in Manhattan. Slamming his hand on the desk, he allowed the thirty agents present to feast on his expression before he uttered a word.

Then, slowly, he rose up like a spectre of doom and bellowed:

'What does it take to catch the king of the psychos?! We've got more agents on this little island than there are stars in the damn Milky Way!'

'He's gone quiet for days now, sir,' said Special Agent Spitz limply.

'I know he has. Everyone knows that. And that's what's killing them. My guess is that he left town long before we got up here.'

Marris looked over at the director.

'Sir, with respect, I believe Kaine's still in New York. I can feel him here.'

The director slapped his fists together as though spoiling for a fight.

'You're pushing me to the limit, Marris!'

'Believe me, sir. Escape would be too easy. This is his turf, and running away just isn't his style.'

'So?'

'So, he'll strike.'

'When?'

'Soon.'

'What's he waiting for?'

Special Agent Marris wiped the perspiration off his upper lip. He sighed.

'For something fun,' he said.

The director regarded him with incredulity.

'*Fun?*'

'Yup.' Marris sighed again. 'The city's locked down and it's dead through and through. Kaine's the kind of man who enjoys the cut and thrust of action, the cloak and dagger, the—'

'Shut the hell up, you imbecile!' ordered Griff.

Special Agent Spitz looked down at her phone, reading a tweet that had just come through.

'You're gonna love this, sir,' she said.

'Huh?'

'In a stand against Cannibal Kaine, New York Fashion Week has just announced that they're going ahead with the shows.'

Every agent present, including Griff, screwed up their face.

'Are they out of their minds?' whimpered Marris.

'They say they won't be silenced,' Spitz replied, 'and it seems as though all New Yorkers are falling in line behind them.'

Agent Marris closed his eyes and thought for a moment. When he opened them again, he was smiling.

'This may give us the break we need,' he said.

Ninety-four

FOR ANOTHER WEEK Kaine stayed in the bedsit. He spent the days writing a manifesto for his brave new world. It ran to more than three thousand pages, and was a wild accumulation of thoughts and experiences.

There were passages of extraordinary poetry and examples of pure genius, and many more that were interminable rants against a system he believed had become corrupted at the core.

Outside the building in which he was holed up, the streets were all but deserted. The only vehicles were those of the police and special forces. There were almost no pedestrians at all. A few supermarkets were open for a couple of hours a day, and they were protected by military personnel. Much of the city had been evacuated. Anyone with the means to get out had been encouraged to go.

Amadeus Kaine hadn't watched TV in days, because his mind had been on writing and planning.

And on his rituals.

They took up an increasing amount of time each day, and involved counting larger and larger numbers in combinations twice as complex as the day before. He knew there was no sense in them, but felt obsessively that they alone brought harmony to the world, and ensured the next day dawned.

More importantly, though, was the sense that the rituals — what he called his 'musings' — would allow his brave new world to become reality. Without them, he feared that catastrophe would strike and there would be no future at all.

Then, one morning, he noticed the television and he turned it on. There was a news report of a major earthquake in eastern China, but the news anchor dismissed it as a trifling story and returned to the only business that mattered.

Cannibal Kaine.

The eye surgeon listened, gripped by the report. He felt a little proud and a little ashamed — ashamed that the country that had raised him was overreacting so.

The news anchor explained how the Big Apple remained locked down and on high alert, with seventy-two per cent of the population long gone. There were wide shots of uninhabited avenues, streets, and highways, and all sorts of superlatives attached to sentences featuring the name Cannibal Kaine.

Clutching a cushion to his chest, amused that he alone could have caused one of the greatest cities on the planet to be abandoned, the eye surgeon cackled with laughter.

'Hysteria,' he said very quietly, 'I'll use hysteria to get my way in the new world.'

A reporter came into view, apparently standing outside the Lincoln Center on the Upper West Side. She explained how there were no plans to close down New York Fashion Week. At a time when every other function and fixture was long since cancelled, Fashion Week was still scheduled. The show must go on.

Kaine almost did a double take.

What a society, he thought to himself — what a sick, pathetic, wretched society! There was a serial killer on the loose and New Yorkers were planning to parade up and down in frocks?

His back warming with anger, Amadeus Kaine forced his fingertips together and snarled. He was about to turn off the television and go back to his manifesto, when he had an idea.

He would go hunting for some nice green eyes.

Ninety-five

AT DAWN THE next day, a hundred special forces operatives locked down the Lincoln Center. They set up a command post, jamming all frequencies but military channels. No vehicles were allowed to access the area for a mile all around, and pedestrians were permitted only if they had an ID bearing a code that had been arranged that very morning.

All day long the great and the good of the fashion world worked away on their runway shows. There was a definite sense of last-minute rush, tempered with a sense of defiance. Fashionistas wore black armbands for the victims who had suffered at the depraved hands of Cannibal Kaine. Attired in muted colours, they took every opportunity to scorn him, and to sing the praises of their beloved Big Apple.

On the Upper West Side, security was tighter than at any time in the city's history. There were endless rows of razor wire and barricades, ID checks and even retinal scanners.

All through the day, the frenzied preparations worked up into a crescendo. TV satellite trucks had parked around the block, with crews covering the event for its news appeal as much as for its fashion value.

Then, at eight p.m., the first guests arrived.

Some of them came in limos, others in armoured vehicles, and many more were shuttled in by special military teams from secret locations across the New York metropolis.

Confronting the threat of attack, dozens of leading celebrities, politicians, businessmen and social climbers turned up. Seated in the front row, their eyes swathed in bandages, were six of the cannibal's most recent victims from Hollywood's A-list.

At nine p.m., with the great hall full to capacity, the first show took place — that of the leading New York designer Helen May Smith. At the end of it, the audience erupted into a tumultuous gush of adulation, thrilled to have made such a prominent stand against the monster, Cannibal Kaine.

The second show featured half a dozen of Europe's most celebrated models, including Olga Siminovitch. The green-eyed Russian beauty was regarded by the fashion world as the most exquisite woman ever to be born.

Her eyes alone were insured for $80 million.

Wearing a silvery satin gown, ruched at the shoulders with a fire-engine-red hem, she had on her head a little pillbox hat in sapphire blue. As soon as they saw her, the audience stood up and applauded riotously.

As the festivities continued inside, the secret service double-checked the entrances, and ordered the security guards to look out for a man dressed in a kilt and sporran. An overheard line of gossip had been misunderstood. The FBI and the NYPD had got it into their heads that the surgeon may have been planning to turn up as a Scot.

In Marris's mind there was no doubt that Cannibal Kaine would crash the event. It was just a question of exactly how and when he would strike. Using military channel D54, he briefed his agents to look out for anyone in Highland dress.

At the back of the Lincoln Center, the service entrance was barricaded behind three separate security fences. Each one had a different alarm system. And, in an effort to foil the wayward surgeon, the caterers had been changed at the last minute. The new team was ordered to wear red scarlet sashes to which their ID tags had been pinned. They had been selected for their ability to put up with changing circumstances, the firm being popular with the city's consular crowd.

As the third runway show began, a member of the catering team heading to work was relieved of his sash, his tag, and then his eyes. But despite having craved them, Kaine spat them out into his hand.

That afternoon, he had shaved his head and managed to get his hands on a theatrical wig. It was shoulder-length rust-red, and somehow seemed to completely alter the structure of his face.

Undressing as inconspicuously as he could, the surgeon put on the catering uniform. Approaching the first retinal scan entry frame, he pushed the eyeballs in front of his own. Grimacing, he managed to get them to stay in place while the machine scanned the retinas.

A high-pitched electronic alarm sounded fast, and the barrier slid open.

Kaine whipped out the eyes, put them in his mouth, and swallowed them.

A moment later he was accosted by a guard who held up his hand.

'I need to do an explosives check, sir.'

'OK.'

The guard held out his hand, motioning for Kaine to step forward into another frame.

'It's gotta go beep,' he said. 'You can't come through until it does.'

Kaine cleared his throat.

'I'll give it another try,' he replied cheerily, stepping back.

'You do that.'

The guard reset the system. Kaine stepped forward.

There was a long pause.

Then a short beep.

'You're good to go,' said the guard.

Ninety-six

REACHING THE INTERIOR of the Lincoln Center, the surgeon was overcome by a warm, fuzzy feeling, as though he were really part of the catering team, a team that actually valued him. For some minutes he went about the chores expected of him — stacking plates and getting the hot canapés out of their cartons and onto serving trays.

Then, as he laid out a tray of Champagne flutes, he overheard one of the caterers talking to another.

'I hear she's a dream,' said the first.

'Who?'

'The Russian one.'

'Which one?'

'Olga…'

'*Olga?*'

'Olga Siminovitch. She's got the most incredible eyes.'

At that moment there was a thunderous cheer from the hall.

'They're applauding her,' said the first caterer. 'I'd give my front teeth just to see her.'

A minute later the applause got even louder, and the fashionistas at the front started dancing with delight. The caterers melted into the shadows and Kaine slipped away into the back. Climbing through a small square window, he emerged in the female restroom. A blonde model was in there doing lines with a friend. Before they could protest, Kaine had broken their necks.

Then he ate their eyes.

After that, he counted to sixty very slowly in multiples of three. The numbers calmed him, as did the rush of Scandinavian eyes.

As he stood there, a third model walked in. She was dead by the time she reached the mirror, beneath which her friends already lay. When he was done with her, Kaine washed his hands three times fast. Slipping out, he skipped over to the end of the runway.

In his hands was a tray piled with tall stems of chilled Veuve Clicquot. Turning his back for a moment, Kaine gulped one down and allowed the bubbles to fizz at the back of his throat. He served a few of the models, and winked at a couple more.

Then he saw her.

Olga Siminovitch.

He knew it was the Russian because her face was more perfect than any other he had ever seen. She had high cheekbones, full wine-red lips, and the skin of purest alabaster.

And her eyes — oh, her eyes.

They were a deep shamrock green, a colour so rare that as an eye surgeon even Kaine had never once come across it before. He looked at her, unable to unlock his gaze.

She smiled.

'Champagne?' he said.

'No, thank you. I've got to go back on in a minute.'

'A pity,' said the doctor. He breathed in very slightly, smelling her. 'Go on,' he said playfully, 'I won't tell.'

Olga giggled, touching an index fingertip to her mouth.

'Promise?'

'Yeah, I promise.'

As she picked the glass, Kaine leaned in. Dropping the tray, he forced her down on the ground and leapt onto her, his mouth lurching to her face.

In terror, Olga squirmed and kicked. She tried to scream, but no one heard.

And then, with the applause erupting again from behind, three shots rang out.

Amadeus Kaine slumped face down.

As he did so, Special Agent Marris vaulted forward and pulled the Russian supermodel to safety.

Ninety-seven

A FULL MEDIA circus ensued.

Every news channel on the planet featured the story of Cannibal Kaine's capture. In an interminable media fest, there were timelines and expert analyses galore, re-enactments and eye-witness interviews, soul searching, laughter, and tears. There were even discussions with the few sightless survivors who had escaped death at the hands of the inimitable Amadeus Kaine.

Among them was an A-list actor, a household name. Having been relieved of his pale blue eyes during the doctor's infamous Upper East Side attack, he refused to go into retirement. After months of recovery and therapy, he went on to win an Oscar for his portrayal of a blind union rights leader from Detroit. The role was just one of many that had been rewritten in Hollywood for the sudden abundance of sightless actors.

As for the streets of New York, they were bustling and alive again for the first time in months. With the threat of Cannibal Kaine nothing but a fading memory, and oculosis resigned to the annals of medical history, life got back to normal.

Special Agent Marris left the service, and moved to New Zealand with his wife and son. He couldn't help thinking of the surgeon, but couldn't bear living on the same landmass either. Having purchased a small patch of green on the North Island, he turned his hand to poultry farming.

After what was billed as the 'trial of the century', Amadeus Kaine was sentenced to ninety-nine sequential life sentences. Preoccupied by multiples of three, he was amused and strangely satisfied by the length of the sentence.

During the trial, the prosecution estimated that he had killed at least three hundred and fifty people, and had eaten in excess of two thousand human eyes.

Defending himself, the disgraced surgeon regarded the jury courteously and said:

'I am aware of the contempt with which you regard me, but for the record I should like to draw your attention to the fact that green eyes make for quite the most delicious low-calorie snack!'

The judge struck the gavel down three times, and Cannibal Kaine was dragged out of the dock.

Ninety-eight

WHEN THE TRIAL was over and the surgeon had been taken away, the satellite trucks, the reporters, and the throngs of curious onlookers dissipated. A great deal of political wrangling followed, which went right up to the White House. It was decided to incarcerate Cannibal Kaine in the solitary confinement Special Housing Unit of the McCreary Penitentiary, Kentucky.

Withdrawing into the twisted maze of his mind, the eye surgeon spent his days rocking back and forth while reciting at lightning speed what the guards assumed was poetry. His lips never ceased moving, although no words were audible.

Then, on one occasion in the first six months, a local Republican politician visited the prison and asked to be taken to see the legendary Dr. Kaine. The hatch was opened and the senator peered in. He saw the inmate sitting there, rocking and reciting.

Clearing his throat, and then taking aim as best he could, he spat. The glob of phlegm hit Kaine on the face, but it didn't break his concentration. His lips just churned the words more frantically.

The only thing was, though, that they weren't words.

They were numbers.

Cannibal Kaine was almost done in counting to fifteen million in multiples of three.

Ninety-nine

SIX WEEKS AFTER the senator's visit, a medical examination suggested that the patient was in withdrawal from not having recently consumed any human eyes.

In one test, a bull's eye was placed in a kidney dish and in front of Kaine. Although the inmate never once ceased his recitations, he drooled openly like a mongrel taunted with a good meaty bone.

The medical officer had advised that he be put on suicide watch. His few belongings were checked twice daily, and a mild sedative was added to his food.

Indifferent to the meals served up through the inspection hatch, Kaine left them most of the time. Within seven months of incarceration, he had lost more than half his body weight. But weight was the last thing on his mind.

All he could think about was his counting.

Nine months after arriving at the drab solitary confinement cell, the guard brought Kaine something special. It was a postcard from New Zealand. The picture on the front showed a Maori warrior with a tattooed face. The scribbled message on the back read:

Don't wish you were here! Marris.

Two months later, a pair of guards arrived at the cell and chained Kaine, as though he were going to be transported. Manacling him, they cuffed his hands behind his back and muzzled his mouth.

And all the while he counted.

'You've got a visitor!' growled the taller one.

Five minutes later, the surgeon's nostrils picked up the scent of perfume. It was one he knew — Chanel No. 5.

The door was unlocked again and an attractive middle-aged woman entered. She had dark-blue eyes and the kind of face that puts a stranger at ease.

But she was no stranger.

'Hello Amadeus,' she said in a flat voice.

Kaine looked up, his lips juggling millions, his eyes wide.

He froze.

'Fran… Francine,' he whispered.

His ex-wife broke down. She was about to call the guard, but something stopped her.

'Why… why did you do it?' she said.

The surgeon didn't reply. He just sat there on the cheap wooden chair, staring blankly.

A guard appeared with a polystyrene cup of tea, the top of a teaspoon resting against the rim.

'I brought you this,' he whispered, bending down to her ear. 'Thought it might strengthen your nerves.'

Francine Kaine took a sip. When she had finished the tea, she placed the cup on the floor, nudging it gently into the corner with her foot. Then she dabbed her eyes with a square of French silk.

'I knew you were sick, but this… Oh my God!'

She reached out, the fingers of her left hand brushing her ex-husband's face. She felt his warmth, his anger, his fear.

'I'm going to leave now,' she whispered.

And a moment later, the only hint that she had been there was the faint trace of Chanel in the solitary confinement cell.

And the cup.

One Hundred

HAVING UNFASTENED THE inmate, the guards shut the tempered steel door and locked it down. No sooner was he alone than Amadeus Kaine had the teaspoon in his hand.

Caressing it gently as though it were an object of exquisite beauty, he slid its curved bowl all over his face.

Then, holding it at a distance, he observed his reflection. Although it was distorted, he was fascinated by what he saw.

And by his eyes. His fabulous, bottle-green eyes.

Fifty yards away, down the corridor, the duty guard turned off the lights for the night. It was 4.35 p.m. Signing the clipboard with a scribble, he slumped into his chair. He was about to say something to the other duty guard when he frowned.

'Didn't you take in a drink to that woman?' he said.

'She's the ex-Mrs. Kaine. Imagine what a fruit loop she must be to have married a psycho like that!'

'Didn't you take in a drink?' said the first guard, repeating himself.

'Yeah…'

'Well, the cup didn't come out. Must still be in there!'

A look of terrible dread descended over both the guards' faces.

They leapt up, grabbing the keys.

As they did so, a torturous exclamation of agony surged down the stone corridor.

Rocking back and forth in the darkness of his cell, Amadeus Kaine swallowed hard.

Then he began counting again.

Finis

A REQUEST

If you enjoyed this book, please review it on your favourite online retailer or review website.

Reviews are an author's best friend.

To stay in touch with Tahir Shah, and to hear about his upcoming releases before anyone else, please sign up for his mailing list:

✉ http://tahirshah.com/newsletter

And to follow him on social media, please go to any of the following links:

🐦 http://www.twitter.com/humanstew

📷 @tahirshah999

f http://www.facebook.com/TahirShahAuthor

▶ http://www.youtube.com/user/tahirshah999

𝐏 http://www.pinterest.com/tahirshah

g https://www.goodreads.com/tahirshahauthor

http://www.tahirshah.com